AT REALITY'S EDGE

A COLLECTION OF SHORT STORIES

BY BEN SOTO

AT REALITY'S EDGE
COLLECTION ONE

First Paperback Edition: February 2024

ISBN 978-1-7321851-7-3

This is for my father, Emiliano Soto, and my uncle Benjamin Soto II. These men helped foster my creativity and pushed me to keep going.

Table of Contents

STAN THE MAN

STORY 1

MY BIRTH NAME is Stanley Waldon the Third. Stan for short. The kids in school used to call me Stan the man. I hated it, but they called me it, anyway. "Stan the man here, just pissed his pants in front of the entire school!" "Stan the man got caught eating glue!" "Stan the man has cooties!" Kids are awful. I never once heard a "Good job, Stan the man!" So, it's not surprising the same nickname found its way into my current job or any other place I found employment. It rolls off the tongue. You can't help yourself, like when you're tickling someone and they want you to stop, but you keep going. People think it's funny or that they're being real clever by saying it. I never thought it was funny. Or clever. It loses its novelty after someone says it to you for the thousandth time.

I started cleaning offices downtown only a couple of weeks ago. It's in the Waramount Solutions building, but you already knew that. I'm not the smartest man, but they do a lot of research and development. It's a decent enough job and pays decent, considering I only clean the place. I take out the garbage, vacuum the offices, mop, dust, and all the other janitorial duties. It was smooth. I had my routine, and nothing went wrong. That was my problem. I got too damn comfortable again.

So much time has passed since the last time — I just didn't think it would happen again. It's what *he* wanted me to think — the bastard! I quit my previous job because of *him*. I moved to another state because of *him*. It's not the first time I have had to do that, and I have a sick feeling it won't be the last. I know it won't be the last.

I used to work in Michigan a few years back. Rose City. It was another janitor job, like this one, but for a smaller company. Best job I have ever had. I won't bore you with all the details, but I did the work that most well-to-do people think is beneath them. Most of the employees in the office see me, but they don't *see* me. Most don't even say good morning back to you if you say it to them. It's like you don't exist. Do you have any idea what that does to a person over time? People are so rude, especially people in fancy suits who are always running around with their espresso drinks, making deals, and whatnot. But Kara — she was different from the rest of those stuck up I'm better than you types.

I enjoyed cleaning her office the most. It always smelled like her — that scent — her fragrance... just heavenly. When I close my eyes and focus real hard, I can almost pick up the subtle hints of the perfume mixed with her natural odor. I understand how weird this sounds, but she always smelled real good.

She took fantastic care of herself, too. The pictures of her and her family always showed her being so happy. She made happiness contagious — like she spread hope. She always smiled at me and said good morning before I could say it to her. Beat me to it every single time.

And then she'd ask about me, and I would fill her in. I never had anything fun to talk about. My life is boring. She listened all the same. She listened! I existed! I'd ask about her day, and she would vent about her husband and kids — good and bad stuff — typical family shenanigans. She was always so lovely and so beautiful. The prettiest dark brown hair you ever laid your eyes on, too. Just perfect, along with those eyes. Those blue eyes that were always so sincere...

One morning, she didn't bother coming in. I noticed right away. It didn't feel right. It felt like something was wrong, not like she called in sick, but like something terrible had happened. The same day, I experienced a horrible headache, and I blacked out that night like I often do. I took it as a bad sign, but let it be. The morning after, Kara didn't make it to work again. Next thing you know, an entire week flew by without her in the office. People got worried.

After that first week, a detective came in asking everybody all kinds of questions about who saw her last, where she was, and whether she had any known enemies. I remembered all those crime shows. I thought of the husband; they always say it's usually someone the victim knows, like the husband.

The detective skipped right over me. I guess that's the best thing about being me. Nobody ever notices you. Nobody bothers to. To these people, I'm just a prop, a thing. I clean the place where they work every single day. To them, I don't have a proper job. I'm part of the facility. A lucky stiff who gets to be the perk of making sure all the offices are spotless and tidy, so they don't have to. An odd sense of relief washed over me at not being noticed by the detective. I didn't know why. Why was I relieved the detective didn't bother asking me anything? I knew nothing.

Later that night, after work, *he* contacted me. I happened upon a note clear as day on my kitchen table. The back door to the lower half of the duplex I rented creaked from the slight gusts of wind hitting it. *He* left it open on purpose. In the note, *he* told me to be somewhere and to make sure I made it on time. The note said he had Kara and that if I didn't show, *he* would kill Kara. I was to come alone, and no cops.

I could have ignored it. The entire scenario was real strange. I didn't have a choice, though. The headaches were getting worse. The blackout happened again the same night, and I couldn't remember a single thing after it. But I did what the note said. Kara needed me to.

The sonuvabitch led me to some apartment somewhere I'd never been before. It was a real nasty place. Abandoned from the looks of it. Garbage was tossed about like every spot was a smaller version of a dump site. Rats ran around like they were training for the Olympics. Even the homeless degenerate bums came across as too good to call this place home.

The pungent odor of urine and shit filled my nostrils when I walked closer to the building that marked X on the map *he* gave me. The stench grew stronger when I stepped inside. It made me feel so damn sick to my stomach. As I walked into one of the far rooms, as directed, I picked up the scent of something else entirely. It was so strong. I will never forget it; it is a smell that has become as natural to me as breathing.

A surreal euphoria held me in place for a while. I didn't move. I was scared. I understood as soon as I set foot inside that room, I would cross a line, and it would change my life forever. My instincts told me to turn and run, but I fought it. A part of me needed to know that Kara was okay. When I turned the corner, I found her. Kara was naked and strung up like a morbid art project on display.

Chains ran from the ceiling, holding up her arms by the wrists. The shackles looked old, and the blood from her wounds mixed with the reddish rust. The support beams the chains attached to were strong. They held her up effortlessly. The shit and urine that evacuated her body after she died sat in a pile below her. The urine dried, but the overpowering niff baked into the floor. She'd been dead for a while. A deep indentation highlighted the skin around her neck like a thin string or wire had choked her. The blood from the wrists was because of the shackles. Other than that, she appeared pristine — angelic. She remained a thing of beauty. Her naked, pale skin glowed in the moonlight, shining through the only open window in the room. Her eyes remained deep, but they weren't sincere anymore. They came across as scared. She died afraid.

I should have called the police immediately and told them about the note, but I didn't. Something inside held me back. Someone was watching me. Someone killed someone I knew and wanted me to know about it. This asshole, whoever *he* was, got *his* sick jollies off it. I left her. I was too afraid to move closer to the body. I'm sorry Kara stayed that way. I have no idea how long it took for someone to find her, either. I just left. I didn't look back. I wanted to leave it all behind me. But my luck wouldn't hold up.

It happened again just as I was getting comfortable. It happens every time I let my guard down! When Paul died, I realized the truth. Paul was a guy I worked with at my last job. He was a genuine friend. Probably the only one I've ever had. He was friendly, the kind of nice you pray for when you're down on your luck. He was the type of guy who would give you the shirt off his back — God's honest truth. He did the training at my last job.

We went out for a few drinks one night after our shift. There was a little corner bar he liked to go to, and it was a great place to relax after working second shift. He was a regular, and they all knew him. The bar staff and locals treated me like I was one of them for a change. The feeling of belonging is powerful. It made me happy. Plus, *he* hadn't shown up for a while. I thought I lost him, but I let my guard down. It happened again. This time was different, though. This time, *he* wanted to show me more than just another dead body. *He* wanted to show me the truth of it all.

The blackout hit, and when I came to, Paul was dead right in front of me. His head was smashed wide open, and blood touched everything in the apartment, especially the places close to Paul's body. *He* had never killed a man before. It had always been women, and it had always been by choking them with some kind of thin wire. Paul's death was so much more brutal. There was jealousy behind it; it was like *he* didn't want me to have a friend.

As I took in the bloody mess surrounding me, a voice spoke up in my head. It wasn't my voice. It was *him*. He laughed at me, and he wouldn't stop laughing. I realized I had something in my left hand. It was a bloodied hammer. The fear coursing through my body kept me from moving, and *he* knew that. *He* taunted me. I remember his voice. It was so cold and dark, and it seemed to be everywhere as I stared at Paul's corpse. He said, *You did this, Stan. Stan the man. I can make you do anything, Stan the man.*

I wanted to yell. I wanted to scream, but nothing came out. I didn't move. I killed Paul, but the voice told me it was *him*. *He* said he needed to do it. *He* didn't like too many people knowing who I was and that all the deaths in the end were for my own good. *He* told me I should thank *him*! *He* protected me and kept people from getting too close because if they found out what I really was, I would be in trouble, and he wouldn't let that happen. Can you believe that?

I ran from the apartment. I ran like before, moving to a new city, getting a new identity, and blending into the background. It was what the voice wanted. If people didn't know me and continued to ignore me, then it made it easier for him to kill. Now, I understood how wrong it was, and I wanted to stop it. But I did nothing.

Mary, the thing is, if I turn myself in, *he* will kill me. I will blackout, and that will be the end. If I did something honorable and whatnot, like ending my life, then I'd still be dead. The truth is, I don't want to die. And for me to live, so does *he.*

Oh, Mary, I'm so sorry. I know you don't believe me right now, but I really am. Ahhh! My head! You don't have a lot of time left, Mary. I can feel him coming. I'm about to black out. It hurts so much when it happens. I...

* * * *

Stanley Waldon the Third stood atop the rooftop of one of the many buildings downtown. The night air gave off the aromas of a busy city, and the smog from the factories kept the stars hidden. He turned to face his latest victim, Mary.

Mary sat tied up and huddled in a corner behind him. Dried mascara tears clung to her cheeks, and she still wore the casual business attire she meticulously picked out for work earlier in the morning. The woman struggled to break free of the ropes binding her ankles and wrists. Stan smiled from ear to ear; he remained confident Mary's restraints wouldn't give. On this night, Stan, the man, would receive another notch on the belt.

"Good old Mary, it is nice to see you again. Stan has left for the moment, but don't worry. I'll be here to keep you company. My lovely little secretary, we'll get to know one another well." Another terrifying smile of sadistic joy spread from ear to ear on Stan's face as he approached Mary during her last moments of life.

BREAK ROOM TALK

STORY 2

"KOBAYASHI. FOR ME, it always starts and ends with him. I have no one else to blame but me. Ever since I was a kid, he always got me into trouble. Now I'm suffering the consequences of his actions like always. Kobayashi... Sometimes, I wonder what it would have been like if he hadn't found me. I could've lived an everyday life, but that would've been too boring. No going back, and no regrets!" Jaina explained with a slight southern accent in the breakroom of the twenty-four-hour WallyMart that employed her. She surveyed the empty chairs occupying the tables surrounding her with a lazy eye and tried with a desperate effort not to pay heed to the loud tick-tock of the clock on the clinical-colored breakroom wall.

Attractive and in her mid-thirties, Jaina carried a graceful beauty she hid. Her long dark hair rested on her shoulders in slight curls, and the baggy WallyMart uniform remained one size too big on her frame. She didn't mind covering up the more enticing aspects of her appearance. How most men approached her left her with a sense of disgust for the male half of her species.

A young man named Luke sat across from Jaina. She regarded her coworker as a little brother and experienced a sense of gratefulness for the late-night company on the night shift. Most shifts that went into the midnight hours didn't have much conversation, and having a newbie sitting across from her guaranteed his full attention regarding various topics. Newbies clung to someone established.

"Kobayashi?" Luke's chuckle gave out a pig snort as he found the name curious. "That's a Japanese name. It means a small forest. I'm studying about the country of Japan right now for school. It's a common surname. Is your friend Japanese or something?"

"He's something alright." She unscrewed the plastic cap of the vending machine soda bottle and took a sip. The rush of sugar hit her body with a slight jolt.

Luke brushed a hand through his light brown hair, unused to the uniform. "So, what is he?"

"A handful. He's been the same ever since I was a child — always bothering me and always the same. Same face, same everything. He is best described as a charming dork. He named himself after the stupid test from Star Trek. It's my fault. The Wrath of Kahn movie was on one night, and I couldn't pronounce his real name. So, he let me call him Kobayashi."

"Oh yeah! The Kobayashi Maru!" Luke recognized his eagerness to share this knowledge, and his cheeks flushed red with embarrassment.

"Oh, God. He'd like you. From that alone, he'd be head over heels." She took another sip of her soda and lounged back in the chair. "He named himself after the unbeatable test because he thinks no one can ever beat him."

"I thought it was because you couldn't pronounce his name." Luke corrected.

She sighed. "That's how it started, Luke, but when he found

out what the test was about, he decided it was an amazing fit."

"But Captain Kirk beat the test by changing the rules. He cheated." Luke explained further.

Jaina nodded in agreement. "I tried to tell him the same thing. I'm not keen on Star Trek, but I know that much. He said when he meets his Kirk, it's time for him to return home and stop doing what he does."

Luke's curiosity grew. "What does he do? Where's home?"

"Home? Just about anywhere is home for that guy. What does he do? He gets me into trouble." She sipped her soda.

"You don't seem like you're in trouble." Luke decided.

"Luke." Jaina cleared her throat as she leaned forward, placing her elbows on the table between them. "Nothing is ever as it seems. Our break is about over. How about we get back to it?"

"Okay." Luke monitored Jaina as she slurped up the rest of her soda; she tossed the empty plastic bottle in the recycling bin and let out a loud belch.

"You can go on ahead of me." She gestured for him to move along. "We're not joined at the hip."

"Right." The young man sighed and exited the breakroom.

The rest of Luke's shift flew by with no adverse incidents. Random customers would appear in the early hours to purchase random items, making one question whether humanity would make it into the future. However, the conversation from the breakroom remained lodged in the forefront of Luke's mind. He grew more curious about Jaina's exotic friend Kobayashi and wanted to listen to more stories. Luke was too shy to ask his female coworker outright, but he figured Jaina would explain more tomorrow night during their break.

* * * *

"You've been sitting across from me, eating your food, and staring. Is there something you want to ask me? I'm flattered if you plan on asking me on a date, but I don't think it would be the best idea. You're about nineteen, right? I'm thirty-five. As much as I enjoy the company of younger men, I don't mix work with pleasure." Jaina sighed with a playful smirk as she sipped her soda, set it down, and pulled her long dark hair back in a ponytail.

"What? No... I..." Luke almost choked on his burger as he chewed it. He set the sandwich down and sipped his fruit drink from a bendy straw before continuing; the simple act made him feel more like a child. "No. I mean, you're attractive and all but... I... I wouldn't... but..." He could feel the redness rushing in his face.

"Relax, Luke. I'm just giving you a hard time. What's on your mind, though? You have the appearance of a six-year-old on Christmas wanting to find out if Santa really ate the cookies and drank the milk." She leaned back in her chair.

Luke leaned forward. "I was wondering about your friend, Kobayashi."

Jaina dismissed the awkward tension with a warm and inviting smile. "Me venting about him yesterday stuck in your head, huh?"

Luke nodded. "I'm curious."

She shrugged. "About?"

"You've known him since you were kids, right?" Luke's excitement grew.

"He met me when I was a child." She sipped her soda.

"And you never found out his real name?" He almost forgot his food and took a quick bite, chewing and swallowing in seconds to be free to speak.

"It's too hard to pronounce. I gave up on it a long time ago. You wouldn't have any luck with it either. Trust me. Intonations must be perfect, and it's like you're almost singing the damn thing." She mouthed the name and chuckled at seeing Luke try to make it out.

"How does he contact you? You talk about him like you expect him to show up any minute." He sipped from the bendy straw.

Jaina pointed her finger at Luke with a knowing smile. "That's because I do. I've been waiting here at this WallyMart for about seven months, just working and waiting. It's all part of his plan. He's brilliant, but don't ever mention I said that. It's impossible to keep him humble if you go on complimenting him."

Luke took another bite of his burger, chewed, and swallowed while taking in the information. "You've been waiting?"

She nodded before taking another sip of soda. "Yup. I'm not sure when or how he'll pop up, but this is where it'll happen. He's the type to let you know minutes or seconds before he's about to do something. Although I must admit, working here is much more peaceful than where he previously had me waiting for him."

"Where?" The desire to know drove Luke crazy.

Jaina sipped her soda and said in a casual tone: "Istanbul."

Luke choked on his food. "What?! That's crazy!" He said after regaining his composure.

"God's honest truth." She held up her hand.

"What were you doing in Istanbul?" Luke couldn't believe it.

Jaina's smile beamed. The burden of hiding her exploits had been challenging, and she wanted to share. "Istanbul is an ancient city; lots of history. I was traveling with Kobayashi and a few other people. He claimed the others to be unique, like me. We had a lead on something he'd been tracking down."

"Which was?" Luke blamed being on third shift for his insatiable need to believe her story.

Her eyes widened, happy to share. "The Ark of the Covenant."

Luke choked on his burger again and, this time, spat it out after a fierce coughing fit. His chest puffed, and he released a heavy sigh once he regained composure with a few sips from the bendy straw. "Oh, come on! You're full of it! There's no way in hell any of that is true!"

"God's honest truth." She held up her hand.

Something about Jaina's body language intrigued young Luke. He could feel her genuine nature pouring through. "Were you watching Raiders of the Lost Ark last night or something?"

"Yes, but that's beside the point. I'm telling you the truth, Luke. We found it, and it was something else. It's not what you think it is from the movies and stories passed on. The truth is always harder to accept once something has been ingrained into a culture. You become so invested in the mythos that the reality is always too shocking or disappointing to handle. Know what I mean? Kobayashi explained as much to me." She shrugged it off.

Luke chuckled, finishing his burger and slurping down the remaining fruit drink. The tick-tock of the clock became noticeable as they sat in shared silence. After clearing his throat, he spoke. "How did this guy meet you? What happened when you were a kid?"

"He kind of found me." She recalled with fondness.

Luke raised an eyebrow. "Found you? Was he a creepy stalker or something?"

She laughed. "Nope. He just found me, Luke. That's the best way to explain it." An intense concentration took hold of Jaina's face. She relived the encounter in her mind. She was a child, and Kobayashi was a grown man. Over all the years, he never aged once. To this day, he remained the same. She focused on Luke, trying to find the easiest way to explain. "He said he'd been searching for me and others like me. According to him, I'm part of an exclusive group of people. He also said my name was fitting because of what it means."

"What does your name mean?" Luke never gave much thought to what names meant.

"The grace of God." She laughed, never having explained it to anyone. "When he first showed up, I was eating candy like kids do – in my room. My aunt left me a bowl of hard candies. While I devoured them, he appeared. I don't remember him coming through a window or opening the door, but he was just there. I threw the bowl of hard candies at him. He laughed it off, and then I just felt safe. You could feel his intentions, which weren't bad or anything. I know this sounds crazy, but I've never been able to talk to anyone about this without sounding like a loon. It's the God's honest truth, Luke. Thanks for at least listening to me right now without too much judgment."

Luke nodded, understanding the sentiment. "No problem, Jaina."

Luke remained silent for the rest of the break, allowing Jaina to relive her past, whether or not he believed it to be true. He gathered from her posture that she relived her previous experiences with the mystery man, Kobayashi. The rest of the shift after their break remained quiet. The late-night hours turned into early morning hours as they carried out their final work duties, and Luke and the "grace of God" went home.

* * * *

Having to sit in the breakroom alone seemed wrong to young Luke. He sat in the same chair, at the same table, and stress ate his burger, awaiting his coworker to appear and share more of her stories. However, he also sensed that something was off with Jaina as they began their night shift at the twenty-four-hour WallyMart. While working on the floor restocking various items, Luke studied Jaina's anxious anticipation. She was more alert and aware of her surroundings than usual and inspected the inside of the store as if something dramatic would transpire at any minute.

Then, Jaina burst through the breakroom doors with the same energy that encapsulated her shift. "Trust me when I say you don't want to sit there!" She barked the words at Luke. The loud tick-tock of the clock filled the air as he responded with silence. Jaina took it upon herself to grab the clock. Without hesitation, she smashed it against the brick wall near her, gratified as the tick-tock noise faded into silence. "I've been waiting to do that for the last seven months. That damn thing drove me crazy."

"What's going on?" Luke grew concerned when Jaina pushed aside the table where they would sit on break on a typical night; Luke's lunch flew about the room as the table wobbled and tipped on its side from the force. She pulled Luke from the wall near that table and positioned him beside her.

"Kobayashi will be here soon. That item he was looking for before we got here, well, he found it again because it got lost in transit. The problem is that other people noticed. So now these people want it, and they aren't good people, and Kobayashi is in a rush to escape with the item in question. So, time is kind of important right now." She gestured for Luke to give her a nod of understanding.

"What?!" Luke stared at his lunch strewn about the break-room floor; the burger contents had splattered everywhere as if the sandwich had exploded. "I was going to eat that!"

"More time for food later," Jaina assured him.

"And what the hell was he looking for? I don't understand what you're talking about! And the new manager is going to be pissed! It's a mess back here!" Luke removed a pickle stuck to his shirt and threw it on the floor.

"Remember when I told you about the Ark of the Covenant? Well, he found it again. He had it, it got lost, and he has it again. Other people want it and are trying to track him down. Follow?" She waited for a response.

"This is fucking crazy!" Luke walked back toward the table to lift it up. "And I have to go find more food now, thanks to you!"

"I wouldn't stand there!" Jaina pulled Luke back again.

"Let me go!" Luke's anger deflated as he heard the engine of a heavy truck approaching their location from outside the break-room wall facing the parking lot.

"Now is an appropriate time to stand back!" Jaina shielded Luke with her body as an oversized brown UPS truck plowed through the cinder blocks. Rubble and debris scattered every which way, and the vehicle's headlights remained on; the beams of light highlighted the dust and powdery aspects of the rubble floating about post-collision.

"Now that was fun!" a boisterous male voice yelled with glee from within the truck. He stood from the driver's seat as if it were just another delivery while running a hand through his short blond hair. Then, following proper parking procedure, the man turned off the headlights, set the UPS truck into park, and turned off the engine.

Luke studied the stranger, taken aback by the perfection of the human form this man represented. The mystery man stepped from the truck and stood before him and Jaina as the ultimate specimen. His smile of greeting accentuated the angelic features of his face, and his bright green eyes took in every aspect of the room. His simple black clothing seemed normal enough, but upon closer inspection, it exuded an exotic aura that seemed alien to Luke.

"Who....? What....? Where...?" Luke stumbled for words.

"Throw out a why and a when, and you're on your way to becoming an investigative journalist. The 'who' part of this I can answer. The name is Kobayashi. I'm sure my associate explained as much. I also have the 'where' covered. We are in a Center Dot breakroom." Kobayashi answered.

"WallyMart breakroom, and that's Luke." Jaina jumped in.

"Same difference, and it's a pleasure to meet you, Luke." Kobayashi smiled at Jaina. "We should go. The contents of the Ark are with me; we don't want that falling into the wrong hands."

"Go? Go where?" Luke began shaking from the adrenaline. "This is batshit crazy! No one has the fucking Ark! It's not even real!"

"But I do have it, Luke. That's the 'what' part to all of this." Kobayashi smiled his perfect smile and walked closer to Jaina. "Sorry that it took me so long."

"Seven months is about the norm." She smiled back.

Kobayashi studied the room and returned his gaze to Jaina. "WallyMart? This is where you worked?"

She crossed her arms, stressing her defensive posture. "It was the best lay-low kind of job I could find on short notice, and it kept me close to my new friend Luke here. That was the plan, after all."

"If you have it, then I want to see it." Luke stood firm with arms crossed, scared and fascinated.

"It's too unstable for you to view. The energy it puts out is vast. I removed it from that silly Ark and placed it in a proper containment field. It's far easier to transport this way." Kobayashi pulled out what appeared to be a flat black disc from his back pocket. The flat surface popped into three dimensions, and a sphere hovered over his right hand. "Within this field are the contents of the Ark. My people lost it long ago when they crashed on your fledgling planet."

"What?! How are you doing that?" Luke walked closer to the black sphere. "Something is inside that thing?"

"Yes. It's a potent energy source. It would tip the balance of power on this planet if discovered and exploited. A long time ago, my people crash-landed on Earth. They found a wandering tribe in the desert and instructed this tribe on how to contain this energy source. They used the primitive technology available mixed with the technology of the crashed ship. In my people's defense, they had no idea that world religions would be started over this."

"Are you telling me you're a fuckin alien?!" Luke laughed with hysteria. "You're crazy! You're just a crazy asshole that crashed a stolen UPS truck through a wall where I work! I didn't even get to finish my food!"

With a stern grasp, Kobayashi took hold of Luke's head with his left hand. The transfer of information was intense and sudden. Luke found himself filled with knowledge and memories regarding the origins of Kobayashi and his people. The species varied in form over the years; appearing as a human was one of their tricks. Luke held his head in amazement once the connection was severed.

"Intense, huh?" Jaina smiled. "Imagine having all that information in your head when you're a little kid."

Luke stared at the two of them in awe. "It's true. All of it. That thing... It's..."

"The Philosopher's Stone. Also referred to as ORME. You have so many names for things that it's hard to keep up. As I've said, my people didn't intend to have a world-impacting religion created over such a thing, but then again, humans are fascinating like that. As a species, your stories tend to become so ingrained and real, even when they can't be true. Your capacity to believe and accept is amazing. It can lead to beautiful discoveries. It can also be detrimental. Then again, that's the dichotomy of being human." Kobayashi sighed, having given this much thought over the centuries.

Luke held his head as if the newfound knowledge would escape if he didn't hold on to it. "You tracked down Jaina and others like her. Why?"

"Say you lost something long ago, and it would take someone several thousand years to find it. Would you trust the language of the time to remain intact? Would any material carrying a message stand the test of time in a violent and ever-changing world?" Kobayashi raised his perfect eyebrow.

Luke shook his head, studying Jaina, who stood with a knowing smile of her own. "No. I guess not."

Kobayashi gave Luke a firm pat on the shoulder. "So, what better way to ensure instructions and a message carry on throughout a long period than to leave it encoded within the DNA of a species? My predecessors, who crashed here long ago, did such a thing with Jaina's ancestors and the others who went with me to Istanbul. This encoding gave me the information needed to track down what you refer to as the Ark of the Covenant. The DNA also carried their last messages. Some were scientific, observational, or personal. One of them left behind a joke that's thousands of years old; it wasn't funny."

"That's incredible!" Luke stepped closer to the two; his comfort with them grew by the second. He watched in amazement as the sphere became a two-dimensional disc again. Kobayashi placed it in his pocket and clapped his hands with genuine excitement.

Sirens blared off in the distance, growing louder as they approached the parking lot outside the massive hole in the breakroom. There wasn't much time left.

"It's time to go." Kobayashi grinned.

"Are you following through with your promise to get me off this rock?" Jaina gave Kobayashi a stern glare.

Kobayashi nodded. "I said I'd show you the stars; there is no time like the present." He regarded Luke. "Are you ready to go with us, Luke?"

"What?" Luke grew confused.

"WallyMart wasn't my first career choice, kid. I got this job here because it was close to where you live. And, yes, I manipulated a few things here and there to get you to work here. Your DNA is like mine. It's encoded with information. It has nothing to do with the Ark, but it is information. Turns out many of his ancestors weren't the greatest pilots and crashed here on Earth." Jaina rolled her eyes.

Kobayashi chimed in. "In defense of my people, all the crash landings did not stem from my race. There are lots of coded messages from other species that couldn't navigate the stars very well either. The technology was new way back then."

"Whatever he says." Jaina smiled at Luke. "So, are you up for going on crazy adventures and getting into trouble because of Kobayashi?"

For the first time, Luke felt an elation of pure joy flood his senses. In the blink of an eye, his life had a purpose, and the universe left him with limitless possibilities. With an eager smile, he nodded to his two new companions.

"Just take my hand, Luke. I'll show you wonders you never even dreamed of." Kobayashi held out his left hand as he placed his right hand within Jaina's.

Luke reached out and placed his hand within Kobayashi's. "Now what?"

Jaina grabbed Luke's right hand with her free one; all three stood in a closed circle. "Close your eyes, Luke. We're about to travel a long distance in a short amount of time."

"I believe that's my line." Kobayashi's tone grew offended.

"I never get to say it." She pouted.

"Because I'm supposed to say that, not you." Kobayashi's tone was adamant.

Luke laughed, ignoring the screeching halt of tires and the blare of more sirens as they flooded the parking lot of the WallyMart. He closed his eyes and opened his mind to the endless possibilities. "I'm ready. Let's go."

THE WATER DRAGON
AND THE CHILD

STORY 3

ANOLE OF THE Emerald Water Dragons emerged from the cool streams of the sun river, whose name derived from the blinding illumination that shot upward from the subterranean cave system of waterways. Anole met the humid temperament of the leafy paradise with contentment as the aromas of verdant flora and earth of the jungle filled her senses with those of wild animals. The humming of cicadas and other insect life, the chirping of colorful avian species, and the random cries of simian creatures drew a stark contrast to the calm waters where Anole spent most of her time.

The Emerald Water Dragons existed as a serene species, but Anole craved the activity of the surface, finding boredom in how her fellow basilisks lived. However, one scent overpowered her. The water dragon did not expect to encounter such an odor so quickly on her journey to the surface world: a human baby. She zeroed in on the toddler as the tiny person stumbled about with the staggered steps of a two-legged creature new to walking.

Anole's presence remained invisible to the human infant; the

Emeralds kept a strict policy of not interacting with the human world while in dragon form. She shook her expansive reptilian wings, and the water sprinkled over the vegetation surrounding her massive serpentine body. Like all her kind, Anole's skills included flight, but that feat stayed hidden, given that the Emerald Water Dragons spent most of their time submerged in the majestic waters below the land. Today was her day to camouflage in human form and walk amongst the Tainakanos. The brown-skinned humans that made the land their home fascinated Anole, especially the adult versions. The toddlers appeared far too intimidating.

She harbored the ability to transform into a human, emulating the land dwellers' physical features and making herself visible to the infant. But then what? Should she care for the creature? Feed it? Did humans eat their young? Anole couldn't recall. The brevity of her studies reflected her impatience; Anole just wanted to reach the surface and walk among them. She performed the duties required by the elders at the most basic levels, but perhaps she should have spent more time reviewing how the Tainakanos dealt with their offspring.

The infant seemed lost as it continued to stumble about, and Anole discovered another scent: blood. The dragon focused on the metallic odor and took light steps around the child, given how massive her quadruped form appeared. She found two adult bodies sprawled on the earth. Humans grew shocked at the sudden sight of their own dead. She remembered that detail during her studies. Curiosity pushed Anole to remain.

Did the toddler belong to the dead Tainakanos? What should she do with the infant? All Anole wanted was to take human form, make herself visible, and partake in the city's culture just beyond the tree line. Now, she was stuck with a random child.

Anole only had hours before needing to return to the illumination of the sun river's depths. The source of life and power for the magic that allowed the Emerald Water Dragons to exist called to her from beneath the water's surface. Too long without the magic would force her to lose her abilities. If she remained in dragon form on the surface beyond the time allotted, her ability to stay invisible would vanish, and she would be stuck in that form, unable to return home. As a hatchling, the elders ingrained cautionary tales into the dragon's mind; the Tainakanos would hunt and kill her for sport. If the time expired while in human form, she would remain a human for the rest of her days.

Anole began the transformation process, allowing the magic to morph her serpentine body into that of a Tainakano. She retained the choice of shifting into a male or female human and decided on the masculine form. Her breathtaking wingspan shortened, and the aqua-green scales of her body molded into dark brown human flesh. Soon, the wings joined with her front legs forming into arms, and she stood upright as the hind legs elongated; the torso readjusted for a vertical posture to accommodate a bipedal stance.

Using her magic, Anole covered the blatant nakedness with the traditional clothing adorned by the Tainakanos. Colorful patterns of fabric covered what their customs deemed inappropriate for public eyes. She made herself visible, and the toddler reacted. The child cried for the first time since she discovered it. This confused Anole, as she figured the infant would have been happy to experience another human.

Anole stepped with ease to the child and lifted it from the earth. The wailing and crying ceased as she held the toddler in her arms, swaying to a pacifying rhythm. The act seemed to soothe the creature and keep more wailing from occurring. This pleased Anole in a way she couldn't describe. She decided the strange sensation had happened because she had shifted into human form. A fine brown cloth wrapped around the infant's bottom, and a small brown and blue tunic covered the top half. Through the smell, Anole determined the creature to be female. Water dragons could tell human sex apart by scent.

From there, Anole headed to the city of the Tainakanos, where she hoped to deposit the child and enjoy her limited time in the human realm. She soothed the child with each step, maintaining a calming rhythm. Another pungent aroma came from the child as she approached the tree line. She expected one of the native Tainakanos might explain the strange odor emanating from the toddler's bottom.

* * * *

"Young man, you should be ashamed of yourself! Your child soiled herself!" The elderly woman, known as Hilda, chided Anole.

Anole wandered through a busy market in Tikalmuka, eager to experience the abundant festivities and exchanges in the city. She figured the dense, populated area would produce a means to deposit the tiny human, allowing her enough time to partake in what the market offered.

"Can you fix her?" Anole asked absentmindedly. She grew more preoccupied with the goings on of the busy market, and she emulated just the right amount of bass in her voice. She heard and studied a few male Tainakanos speaking before attempting to communicate.

The elder woman tisked placing the child on a table meant for preparing her goods. The old Tainakano seamstress owned a fine display of handwoven garments with influences that spanned the kingdom and beyond. Anole gathered, given her old age, that Hilda was well-traveled.

With experience as her guide, Hilda undid the cloth wrapped around the baby's bottom. The piercing aroma forced the old woman back, causing her to knock over a basket of woven tunics she caught at the last minute, and she regained control after a few moments. Then she cleaned the infant's bottom, having the proper means at her disposal. Unfortunately, it wasn't the first time an infant needed help at the market.

She tossed the soiled cloth, the baby laughing during the experience, and wrapped the child up in a fresh one so the cloth remained tight but comfortable. The elder noted how stained the tunic appeared and tisked. "This won't do," Hilda muttered under her breath.

Hilda removed the tunic; she froze. "How did you come by this child?!" she demanded. The friendly demeanor was gone.

"What?" The question confused Anole. "I found her. Why?"

A pendant hung around the toddler's neck. It was the royal pendant.

"Guards!" Hilda cried out, holding the infant close to her and creating space away from Anole, using the tables around her market spot as barriers.

"Guards?" Anole echoed, still confused.

Five intimidating Tainakano men patrolling the market and bursting at the seams with lean muscle approached the table. Their wooden armor appeared minimal; the unique trees of the deep rainforest produced robust and lightweight timber that was easy to mold. The wood could withstand the impact of almost any bladed weapon.

The guard in charge stepped forward. "What is it this time, Hilda?" He asked with a tone that suggested the woman called on them often.

"You must take this man, Technalon!" She pointed at Anole with her free arm; the other one cradled the infant.

"For what crime?" Technalon asked, doubtful the interaction was worth his time.

Anole watched as Hilda held the baby up for the guards to see. The royal pendant hanging around the little creature's neck shined when the sun hit it.

The at-ease guards drew their blades. The tips surrounded Anole's neck, pinpointing where each stood around her. The shocked expressions on their faces soon turned to rage.

Technalon kept his sword in the scabbard on his hip. "Where did you get this child?!" he demanded, spittle flying from his mouth.

Anole realized the masculine form she wore might be too intimidating for her current situation. Attempting to de-escalate the rising tension, she transformed into a feminine shape, the clothing changing to mold the new body.

The guards grew even more defensive, stepping back while keeping their blades on Anole. Again, she grew confused by the hostility. "I found her," Anole said, her voice changing to complement her new form.

"A changeling!" One guard yelled.

"Kill it!" A second one shouted.

"Hold!" Technalon ordered.

The infant wailed with a primordial cry, and a fit like no other took over. Hilda did her best to keep the toddler calm. Others in the market watched with fascination as events unfolded.

"Where did you find the child?" Technalon kept a calm tone. Command came easily to him, and his training helped control his emotions.

Anole explained where she found the child in the most agreeable and cooperative voice, which unnerved everyone around her. Anole did not protest or fight when the guards bound her arms, dragging her to what they referred to as a prisoner's hut. They tossed her into a cell, and she sensed their collective fear of her. She didn't understand. What did she do wrong?

* * * *

Random straw from various batches was strewn about the holding cell along with a bucket for what Anole realized collected the liquid and sometimes solid materials that exited a human's body. The bars on the small window allowed a bit of light to shine through, and she patiently waited. She was not familiar with this particular human custom. Anole could force her way through the bars that kept her in the cell, but she figured that wouldn't be right. How long did she have to wait?

A sudden rustling in the straw startled Anole, much to her embarrassment. She was a dragon, after all. There wasn't much that was supposed to scare her. What surprised her was the figure of a man dressed in unfamiliar clothing, revealing himself from beneath the copious amounts of straw. He appeared to have awoken from a deep slumber. He yawned and stretched, his red trousers and gold button-up shirt stressing how out of place he appeared, along with his pale pink skin.

"Hello there!" His accent differed when compared to the Tainakanos. He smiled with curious eyes and seemed ecstatic about having company. "Does the lovely woman I have the pleasure of rooming with have a name?"

"Anole." She was unafraid but didn't want to be startled again, so she monitored the man.

"A pleasure. My name is Rem Bosker." Rem gave a profound, deep bow to Anole. "At your service."

Anole bowed in return, confusing Rem. He chuckled at the gesture. "It's not the custom for a lady to bow in return from where I hail."

"You are not from here?" She asked.

"Guilty." He smiled again. "I'm from another realm that makes up the Celestial Domain. Another planet, or orb, or sphere, as they are called."

"They don't like you." She stepped forward.

Rem laughed again. "My, you are blunt. That can get you killed in certain areas. I imagine that's why you're here."

"No. I wanted to experience the market." Anole corrected, not catching the humor.

"It appears you didn't make it. The market is closed by now." He sat down in a pile of straw.

"Why are you here?" she asked, emulating the behavior and sitting down.

Rem sighed. "Let's just say I procure rare items not for sale." He smiled. "And someone that didn't want to sell a particular item wasn't thrilled that I was in the middle of a procurement whilst in their residence."

Anole sighed, understanding. "You're a thief."

"That's a rather crass label, but not inaccurate." Rem pouted, crossing his arms.

Anole did the same, hoping to learn something from Rem's mannerisms.

"Get on your feet!" Technalon barked as he entered the prisoner's hut.

Rem darted up to his feet. A split second later, Anole did the same, copying Rem's movements.

"You killed them!" Techalon yelled through clenched teeth.

"I killed no one!" Rem protested.

"Not you, outsider!" Technalon stood on the side of the bars nearest Anole. "Her!" His eyes filled with rage. "The Chief and the Chieftainess were murdered! You killed and spilled royal blood!"

Anole realized why they reacted with such fear and anger. Changing forms from male to female might have been a mistake. That only heightened their suspicions. She locked eyes with Technalon. "I did not." She maintained eye contact.

"We found their bodies where you said you found the child. So why didn't you mention her dead parents?" Technalon demanded.

"It did not occur to me," Anole answered with honest enthusiasm.

"I didn't take you for the murdering type. I must be slipping. I'm such an amazing judge of character." Rem lamented.

"I didn't kill anyone," Anole said again.

Technalon took a calming breath. "We will have two executions this evening. One for the thief and one for the murderer." Technalon stormed off.

"I still think that punishment is a bit extreme!" Rem called after the guard. He turned to face Anole. "You're no murderer." He said after sizing the woman up again.

"Correct," Anole confirmed. "And you are a thief."

Rem sighed and sat back down in the straw. "Indeed. At least my last moments will be in paradise. The weather is always beautiful here, after all."

"I don't have much time," Anole said aloud, noticing the sun's descent through the window bars.

"What do you mean?" Rem asked.

Anole dismissed the question with a hand gesture. If Anole didn't return to the sun river before nightfall, she would be stuck in this realm as a human or a dragon, depending on which form she remained in upon sunset. The magic allowing her to remain invisible would be gone forever, and the Tainakanos would never stop hunting her until they killed her.

* * * *

The procession to the city square, which sat before the royal residence, was met with scorn by the commoners standing off to the sides. They considered the outsider a bad omen, and the death of their beloved Chief and Chieftainess was the result. The strange woman with the outsider was the one who carried out the heinous act of murder and would soon pay for her crime.

"When I first arrived," Rem commented, "they all loved me. I was exotic. The outsider with an accent. Now they want me as dead as you."

Anole gazed at Rem. "What did you try to steal?"

"A royal pendant, one imbued with magic. The one wearing it can have no harm come to them. A useful item if you live a life of danger or have grand ambitions that require bloodshed." He sighed. "I found it in the royal residence, but our guard friend, Technalon, discovered my trespassing."

Anole thought on this. Technalon was nowhere to be seen. She figured he would have been here for the executions, given how outraged he appeared in the prisoner hut. She realized the shock was not of seeing the child, but of the pendant the child wore. Technalon recognized it.

"Are you well?" Rem asked. "Silly question, I know. We're

about to be executed, so I guess it doesn't matter."

"Where in the royal residence is the pendant?" Anole asked.

Rem grew confused about why the young woman wanted to know, but he played along. "In the family room, near the infant."

"Is that where it would be now?" Anole continued her interrogation as they were led to an elevated stage with a chopping block.

"I imagine so. The Chief's daughter would be returned to the residence. A regent is in place until the child comes of age. The pendant will keep that child alive until she comes of age." Rem mused.

"Can you take me there?" Anole asked.

Rem held up his hands, bound in rope. "I'd love to, but we're a little tied up. Have you forgotten?"

Anole studied the ropes that bound their hands, having indeed forgotten. She turned her sight on Rem again. "I'll get us out of here. Can you take me to the child?"

Rem laughed as they climbed up the steps to where two guards waited with sharp swords. The crowd gathered, yelled obscenities, and cheered for the death of the outsider and murderer.

"Can you?" she asked again.

"If you can get us out of this, I'll take you anywhere your heart desires." He promised, amused. The amusement faded as Anole tore from the ropes and ripped the ones holding Rem's hands together.

"Deal," she said in a casual tone. Anole remembered humans needed confirmation of verbal agreements and wished she had paid more attention to those lessons before going to the surface.

Rem gasped as Anole proceeded to change her shape. Her arms split into front legs and wings as she lunged forward, growing in size. The dark brown skin associated with the Tainakanos changed into aqua-green scales, and her wingspan blanketed the setting sun.

The crowd ran in fear. The guards froze, not ready for such

an encounter. Rem laughed as Anole swooped him up with a wing, placing the thief on her back. Then, she flew into the sky toward the royal residence.

* * * *

A mass panic took over the royal residence as news of the dragon spread. Technalon didn't care. He slew the child's protectors and stood over the infant's body, eyeing the desired pendant hanging around her tiny neck. Then, to test the power of the magical charm, he unsheathed his sword and stabbed at the child. The blade stopped, held back by an invisible force. Technalon smiled at this.

Technalon's smile vanished as the wall nearest exploded inward. Debris trickled around him, making a mess of the royal nursery. Toys meant for the infant and lavish gifts for when the child grew older were strewn about in haphazard piles. Then, after regaining his senses, Technalon was shocked to see the dragon eyeing him up.

Rem Bosker jumped down from Anole's back with clumsy grace. "Get away from that child!" Rem demanded, stumbling for balance.

"This isn't your sphere, outsider!" Technalon barked. He kept his sword before him. The might of the wooden armor kept most of the debris from doing harm.

"And that pendant doesn't belong to you," Anole said with her authentic voice. Words came not from her mouth but filled the room. Her voice rang inside the heads of Rem and Technalon.

"Tell me, where did you come from, dragon?!" Technalon demanded.

"This world belonged to us long before humans arrived." She explained, remembering the history of the expansion throughout the Celestial Domain via the portals. "You are the murderer. You killed this child's parents, did you not?"

Rem kept a careful distance, circling around Technalon. The guard noticed this but kept his eyes on the dragon as he spoke. "I did! They were weak! They carried this power at their disposal! This Chief could have used it to conquer!"

"It was not your place to make such decisions." Anole moved closer, her steps light despite the mammoth dragon form.

"And it is your place to mettle with the affairs of the Tainakano?" Technalon countered with indignation in his voice.

This gave Anole pause. Did she have the right? She thought of the infant and how it warmed to her. She thought of the tiny creature's innocence. At that moment, the Emerald Water Dragon decided it was her place to protect the infant.

Anole made quick work of Technalon's defenses, swatting the sword away with her wing, and clenched her formidable jaws around his squirming body. The mighty wood cracked beneath her sharp teeth. Dragons were one thing the wood could not stand against. With ease, Anole tossed Technalon's flailing body through the wall-sized opening her abrupt arrival created, and he fell to the streets below. The distant audible thud of his body's impact confirmed the man would cease being a threat.

"Well. It's not every day a dragon comes to my rescue." Rem gave Anole a deep bow; this time, he meant it with the greatest respect he could muster.

Anole moved with grace toward where the infant lay. The cradle remained sturdy throughout the violent engagement, and the child laughed with delight and excitement upon seeing Anole's true face.

"I think she likes you," Rem commented.

"I think I like her too." The dragon smiled. "I must go." She turned from the child and attempted to cloak herself. Realization hit Anole. Forlorn dragon eyes peered out the opening where the outside wall once existed and saw the sun disappear on the horizon.

"What's the matter?" Rem asked.

Anole moved to the opening, her impressive dragon head

staring at the vast sky, emoting sadness. "I'm too late. I'm stuck like this forever. Trapped in the human realm."

* * * *

Rem Bosker received a full pardon from the new Regent in charge. She had been most appreciative of his involvement in saving the life of the future Chieftainess and allowed Rem to return to his realm.

After partaking in the luxuries offered by the local government, Rem found himself with a new wardrobe and feeling refreshed. He awaited off-world passage through the travel portal placed here by the Continuum Maximus that allowed for travel throughout the Celestial Domain, and he smirked to himself.

Rem got away with it.

He reached into his pocket and held on to the pendant that granted the owner protection. During the commotion with Anole and the traitor, Technalon, he swapped the true one for a fake, as he always intended to do. The job was completed, and he would take the pendant to the one who hired him.

Rem struggled with removing such protection from the child. Then he peered into the sky and saw Anole soaring through the air off in the distance. The mighty dragon circled the city, and not a single Tainakano lifted a weapon against her.

Who would dare hurt the child, Rem thought, *when a dragon is her pet? No, not pet. Her protector. Friend, even.* Rem laughed, stepping through the portal when his turn came up.

* * * *

Anole found freedom by flying through the open sky. The avian species of the rainforest welcomed the mighty dragon.

Sometimes, they flew alongside her as if she had always been there. Of course, it wasn't the same as navigating the underwater terrain of the sun river, but it would have to do. This was her life now.

She circled the emergence point, where she first arrived on dry land. She flew down, nestling near the water and allowing the shade of the ancient trees to blanket her elegant serpentine body. Anole yawned, stretching out her wings, and looked at the spot where she first set eyes on the toddler. She chose to protect an innocent child, and Anole could happily live with that decision.

BY THE SWORD

STORY 4

EXISTENCE DEPENDS ON the context. What is alive by a particular set of standards is dead by another. The things humans create have life; they have souls. These things do not utter sentences like humans do because this is a human thing. They make us with a purpose, and this purpose gives us life.

Fire forged me.

Controlled chaos enveloped my senses when I realized thoughts belonged to me, and this controlled chaos would define the crux of my existence after my birth. My first master gave me my life; he gave me a purpose. He folded and repeatedly pounded my steel upon itself until he realized my deadly form's perfection. Beauty and death encapsulated my design; one beheld the grace and nature of my purpose.

Once my hard skin cooled in water and dried, the first master added the guard. And what a glorious construction! It combined with my effulgent steel skin in perfect harmony, displaying an elegant dragon composition fit for a true warrior. The collar, handle, and black braid to follow all complimented the sleek architecture of the golden guard. Even the butt cap or kashira, as spoken in the human tongue, resonated with resplendent style. Ostentatious ornaments decorated the handle, and when my birthing process concluded, I had never experienced a higher level of unification.

The master of my creation held me before him and granted me my first slices through the air. I flew through the wind, cutting the air, and he commanded me with an all-knowing sense. His hands passed upon gratitude and satisfaction like none other. The master grew so overjoyed with me! In truth, he held me and practiced with me more than any other swords that came before and, I say with confidence, any to come after.

The first master transported me to my counterpart, where I would slumber, my saya or scabbard, until my need as a warrior arose. My loving shelter... It appeared black to the pitch, with two golden dragons etched on both sides made of thin golden lines. The sageo and kurikata leading to the scabbard mouth, or koiguchi as I've known it — live in my mind as inviting and beautiful as the flesh and blood of an enemy ready to die.

With reluctance, I passed on from the first master of my creation. Through his touch, I experienced a profound sense of sorrowful loss. This remains the only time I would ever encounter such emotions from any that held me, and it remains the only time I wished to stay in my scabbard to drown in the joyous and loving hands of the one who created me.

War was imminent.

I do not recall the details, for it happened so long ago. I remember joy; I would soon realize my purpose. I would fight, and I would kill. I would relish in the blood of my enemies as intended and destroy any that would dare block my path. My destiny to be a part of such a thing pushed me to bloodlust. This remains my only true nature. I am an instrument of death, you see.

An eerie calmness blanketed the battlefield as if those present realized most would die; they worked to ignore the notion. Men shouted from one to the other, giving last-minute orders and attending to final preparations. The sudden movement came upon me following that calm, and the chaos of battle caught me off guard at first. With eager determination, I immersed myself in the violent symphony. The bouncing from the creature my master rode — a horse — shook me until the moment of light. The darkness of the scabbard ended, and my steel lay naked to the world. I grew confident in my purpose, and without hesitation, I struck upon the enemy.

My first duty rested with my master. I did my best to protect him, blocking blows from those created to kill as I did. My skills proved superior. I prevented the attempted death blows, and I even shattered weaker opponents. In the haze of confusion, I can't recall which human life ended by my steel. But I remember the mixture of blood that soaked into the essence of my being, and this exhilarated me beyond words. Enemy after enemy went down and died. Sword after sword challenged my might and failed. My war master and I emerged from the chaos unbeatable.

The yells subsided, replaced by the groans of men about to die mixed with the cheers of the victors. I, my master, and those who fought and survived with him remained. We emerged victorious, and the blood from that day gave me something to live for. It came across as cruel the way my war master wiped the precious blood from my blade and placed me back within my counterpart. I looked forward to the idea of battle while I lay in slumber. When the next engagement would occur, it preoccupied me like blue preoccupies the sky on a cloudless day.

Many campaigns and battles followed. Time and time again, the swiftness of my movements defeated my master's enemies, and they perished with extreme prejudice one after another. None possessed the might to stand before us, and none would. Much to my dismay, the time gap between engagements grew, and my slumbers extended. Years would pass until I once again experienced the light.

I remember the last touch of my war master. He held me up, and his hands changed from what I remembered. The once solid and fearless hands I recalled from the first battle vanished. Cold hands replaced them – fragile and unable to maintain a tight grip. Sadness entered my essence, and as the sadness deepened, the old, weak hands pulled me from my scabbard, allowing me the light.

New hands touched me; these hands belonged to the war master's son. My new duty lay with protecting him. I would fight for his honor, and my commitment unto him would be like a mountain upon the earth: unmovable. His hands expressed a delicacy and held me with an immense respect as deep as the respect he harbored for his dying father. The gratefulness and exhilaration of his hands passed to me, and at that moment, I ignored the words spoken between a dying father and his only son. Some things are meant to be ignored.

He practiced much with me, and I did my best to guide him in the proper forms. I spent more time training with him than I did with his father. The relationship satiated some aspects of my being, but I still craved blood and flesh. The contest of battle defined my existence. One fateful day upon a dirt road, the gods would grant my lust for battle, and little did I know the blood spilled would not be my enemy's.

Another man traveled the road between villages. He passed my master with disdain; a quick insult shot from his mouth. Honor being the way, I urged my master to speak up and demand an apology. The enemy would not yield and continued to spew foul vituperation. We attacked first, and the first strike sent the man back with a quick reflex; he smiled as if expecting the move. Before one could breathe, the stranger drew his sword, and it craved blood. Like recognized like.

To this day, the sword held by the stranger remains unfamiliar. The combatant blade exuded wisdom and experience, making me believe it was created before my birth. Blood of countless enemies coated the naked steel over time, and it cried its warnings to me, recognizing the youthful inexperience I protected. I, like my master, did not listen. We would have our blood on this day.

The next strike happened at great speed. The young master used me to execute a graceful block and counterattack. To my dismay, the counterattack failed. The elder blade laughed at me as if knowing I could do nothing to save the young master. I urged my master to go on. I believed I would not fail him.

The duel ended in a heartbeat; most of these encounters finish in the blink of an eye. With a few strokes of a confident blade, the victor lives another day while the loser hopes for an honorable death. He held on to me for as long as his grip allowed after he fell on the dirt road. The man who insulted him trotted off down the path, intent on the business preoccupying him before the encounter, and the elder sword returned to its scabbard after having my master's blood wiped from its blade.

The grip remained determined, like he never intended to let go; I thought he might survive. His hand unclenched; the pressure vanished from his grip as his soul fled his body. I fell to the dirt road like some mundane object to be tossed aside without care. I yearned only to be held again. I wanted time to reverse so I might redeem myself and protect my master, but I failed. His dead body next to me on the side of the road reminded me of this.

Half a day passed before someone stumbled upon his body on the road. This man lived without honor and pillaged through my master's body, searching with desperate determination for anything of value. He lifted the scabbard from the body and lifted me from the ground. I returned to slumber, taken away from the light.

The hands of the thief did not understand grace or gratitude. They lacked confidence and held me like a desperate drunk man trying to hold on to his balance. Those he challenged disposed of him with the ease of breathing, and I cannot say that I experienced sorrow for this or that I even tried to protect the waste of flesh.

More slumber followed his demise. Then, a few more mean-

ingless battles. More people held me, and none gave me the respect I deserved, so as a result, I cared little for their welfare. All
the while, I yearned to be with the original master who created
me in the fires of chaos so long ago. I desired to bathe in his loving grip.

Time flowed like an uncaring river, and I fell into the grip of
my last master. He led a group of bandits with their own code of
right and wrong. My final engagement took place in a forest far
from any homes and far from any roads. The bandits I found
myself attached to understood little of actual fighting, and when
men from the lord's personal estate hunted them, they discovered their pathetic camp. The well-trained soldiers slaughtered
the bandits down to the last man.

The rogue bandit holding me did well enough for one not
trained. He was not ready for a sword like me. I killed a few of
the lord's soldiers, given that his will and determination fueled
some of my skill, but I fell to the ground with the bandit soaked
in blood. Snow fell, sprinkling the forest as he took his last
breaths. The battle continued, and the pure white of nature
mixed into a bloodied crimson by man's insatiable need for violence. Not a single bandit remained alive, and nature buried me
along with the other bodies beneath the falling snow.

Time passed; it always does with indifference. The bodies of
the bandits decayed as the seasons changed, and nature disposed
of and reused them in the forest with her great wisdom. The
ground rose around me as the seasons adjusted. I found myself
buried beneath the earth, never able to speak or be with my saya
again. I yearned for the scabbard that comforted me during my
times of rest. Saya was lost to me, and I became lost in time.

So many years passed.

On one fateful day, the surrounding earth moved. Light
shined down upon my blade, and I experienced the sun's bril-
liance again. I imagined what the world would be like centuries
later. The age I hailed from vanished, and the men who recov-
ered me passed me around like some delicate thing that might
break at the slightest pressure. If only they knew my true glory

and conquest! If only they knew my actual strength!

They took me, cleaned me, and brought me back. My design remained a marvel to gaze upon with loving eyes. As far as I understood it, my purpose continued to be that of a protector and death dealer. Those who unearthed me harbored other plans. They cleaned and treated me well, but their intentions were not for combat. I am a former shell of what I once was, now made to sit on display.

They call this place a museum. The humans collect old artifacts and show them off for those to look upon and study. The age to which I was born was dead, as was my purpose. From those imprisoned with me, I learned of far more destructive weapons created that made the likes of my kind obsolete.

Children pass, adults pass, and they all reach out, wanting to hold me. I can see it in their eyes, but I am behind glass. My purpose now is for amusement, and never again will I experience the hold of a true warrior. Never again would the respect and joy of being held by my creator master or my first war master overtake me. Only by my kind did I know this world, and that was by the sword.

FINAL LETTER TO ANN

STORY 5

IN THE MOVIES, the dying hero talks about how cold it feels. Right now, I'm just numb. It's a numbness reminding me how my time is almost up, and it has nothing to do with the alien terrain surrounding me or the rest of my squad. Death is immanent, and nothing about this mission makes me believe I deserve the title of hero.

Planetary entry is my favorite part of the job. It speaks to the child in me who somehow survived the harsh realities of war. Through the viewport of the dropship, it starts with a fiery streak. A corona of incandescent plasma surrounds the ship in the blink of an eye. The inky blackness of deep space turns into a canvas of vibrant colors; this is the violent reaction of the alien atmosphere as we descend to the surface.

We passed through endless layers of ethereal clouds, each with a unique shape and luminescence. Tendrils of iridescent gas curled around the dropship; I recorded it to share with you. After the clouds, the terrain of the alien environment reveals itself. Jagged mountain ranges, sprawling bioluminescent jungles, and vast oceans present themselves as a surreal dream. They appear familiar yet remain utterly unfamiliar.

The harsh environment runs at extreme temperatures depending on the time of day. The pilot maneuvered through uncertain air currents, employing controlled bursts through the thrusters. The planet's unique gravitational forces and atmospheric anomalies also factored into how the pilot called upon her considerable skills.

We geared up, doing a last check on armor and weapons. The sensation of the landing gear contacting alien ground served as our cue. The silent notion we were marching to our deaths hung in the air. Every time we deployed, we realized it might be our last time, but no one ever believed it. The bay door dropped, and we marched out into the unknown to carry out orders from someone who had never set foot outside an administrative office.

Thoughts are floating through my mind in slow motion. It grants me a sense of peace. I can pick everything I want to remember; that's the power of the cerebral implants we're issued when we enlist and are deployed off planet. Are the implants or my actual brain doing it? I can't tell anymore. Of all the memories I can relive as I fade away, I keep returning to you, Ann. You are all I miss about Earth.

I'm alone on this God-forsaken rock. Is it a habitable planet in a somewhat human-tolerant system? Sure. I guess you can say this holds true in the vaguest of terms. But everything here wants to kill us the way the body's immune system fights off an invading virus. We're not natural here; we never have been. Planet DC22 hates what we are and never wants us to return. It's hard to tell what's more dangerous: the aliens we're fighting or the planet's wildlife.

I'm wounded; it's terrible. The blood... I couldn't stop it from seeping out of my stomach. Their weapons pierced my armor. I tried; I'm too weak to keep fighting, and I'm so tired. Each breath takes so much out of me, and the drastic temperature drop isn't helping either. The pool of blood coming from my body is freezing on the jungle floor. The extremes on this planet are baffling. It goes from heated jungle to frozen jungle, and the life here adapted to it.

Ann. My lovely Ann. I wish I knew you could listen to these last thoughts of mine. I pray to God the transmission makes it from this damn implant in my head and to the ship in orbit and that somehow, you'll understand how much I love you with this message being sent through subspace channels. I never told you that enough, did I? I meant to. I meant to do a lot of things. I guess that's how we're supposed to feel at the end — never enough time.

The bastard shot me. Point blank. The weapons of the indigenous population on this world are like the firearms of the twentieth century on Earth. The material, however, isn't on our periodic table. Whatever they made the projectile bullet from cut clean through the exo-armor meant to save my ass.

I understood the risks of signing up. It was exciting; I admit it. See the stars! Travel through space! Conquer planets in the name of Earth! It became my duty, and I hope you truly understand that. First Contact — it was hard for all of us. The first extraterrestrial life any human encountered ended up being the bully we feared them to be. Half a continent lost in the blink of an eye. But we showed them, didn't we? Human resolve kicked in. Nothing can stop us when we unite for a cause. And look at us now! Earth has conquered 16 systems since the First Contact incident. When will it be enough? When will we ever stop seeing something different from us as a threat? We took it too far. Treasonous words, I know, but I'm dying, anyway. Sometimes, following orders isn't enough. You should ask why. I wish I had possessed the courage to ask that question sooner.

I guess the little sonuvabitch that shot me honored his form of duty as well. I mean, who wants to be conquered? He got the drop on me. I got sloppy, and he took advantage; the exo-armor made me careless. That little alien bastard! So here I am, dying on a planet so far from home — so far from you.

Others are dying around me. Turner lasted for as long as he could. I think he called the ship for air support. The ship should be in orbit above this position soon. Not a lot of time left. I wonder what will come first: death from this wound or death from the shitload of ordinance about to be dropped?

You looked so beautiful the day I left. I told you God and I — we are best buds, and you didn't have to worry. You did your best to laugh, being brave enough for everyone. Ann, you were always the rock. They're all going to need that. They'll all need your strength to carry them through what's coming.

I'm slipping away. It's funny. It's painful, but it's peaceful. Peace exists in this death. It's like when you experience the relief of finishing something hard. It becomes worth it if you hold out for as long as you're supposed to, and that's what I'm doing.

I'm sorry I won't be able to help your dad finish the garage. He was waiting for my sorry ass to return from my "space adventures" so he could show me how a real man builds things, but I won't have the pleasure. He was always such a hard ass and old school to the core. I remember when I asked his permission to marry you. I was so damn nervous, and he just sat in his favorite chair, looking at me like the battle-hardened vet he is. For a second, I thought he would say no, but he stood up, shook my hand, and gave me his blessing. Relief couldn't describe how this simple gesture eased my worry.

I can hear it coming in; there's no mistaking the sound of those missiles breaking through the atmosphere. I guess that answers my question. Nothing for miles will be left when those explosives drop. Us. Them. All gone. That's what the bastard gets for shooting me. He couldn't have gotten too far.

Oh God, they're here. It's so loud... I see the light moving toward me. It's warm... So hot... It's all I see now... And the noise...

Goodbye, Ann. I lov...

* * * *

Ann laughed and conversed with her family for their weekly Sunday gathering when the transmission arrived from the orbiting relay station. She was grateful she listened to it alone in their bedroom; she had been tempted to play it as soon as it arrived for everyone since the entire family was over.

Her nephews and nieces laughed and played, spending equal time in the vast backyard and downstairs recreation room; the smacking of quick feet going up and down the stairs occurred at regular intervals. Her dad argued with her brother about which football team would take the World Super Bowl this year. Her mother spoke on the holoscreen with her aunt about who would host Thanksgiving this year. The world kept going, but for Ann, at this moment, her world had frozen still.

LONG LIVE THE QUEEN

STORY 6

PETER DUMEAUX LIVED his pale-skinned existence for twenty-five years without a single alarming incident or superbly tragic encounter. He was a natural redhead whose origins remained a complete mystery. The identity of his birth parents was unknown to him, and a loving family adopted him and took him in as their own. The foster family gave Peter an identity when he had none, and he remained grateful for the blessing. However, the emotions remained inescapable; Peter was a social outcast, regardless of the loving family. A nagging sensation persisted, screaming he would always be a human defect.

A series of failed relationships followed Peter as anchored baggage. Many times, the awkward youth swore he understood love. Still, the confidence in such a notion dissipated when an authentic opportunity for a long-lasting romantic union presented itself. As time passed, he realized he loved no woman willing

to share his bed for an intimate rendezvous. This scared him beyond measure. It left him empty inside, like an alien looking in.

Having steered clear of college and people, Peter found comfort in obtaining employment that required little to no teamwork.
Carrying out tasks as a solitary individual brought him immense
joy. This created an even greater rift between Peter and people;
human relations grew harder to maintain. His new job lived up
to the meaning of a dream come true. He would work maintenance in a facility during the graveyard shift. There would be little interaction with people, and they would pay him to carry out
tasks alone. He was so beside himself with joy that the excitement kept him awake the day before the first shift.

FIRST NIGHT

"Do you think you get the gist of it?" Andy asked Peter as he
approached the concrete stairway to the facility's basement.

Peter regarded the training technician. The weathered old
man carried much experience under his belt; he paid for this
experience by sacrificing the hair on his bald head through the
stress of gaining it. "I think so. I do my rounds, check the offices
in the administration wing, and watch for and change burned-out
lights around the building. I also try to complete as many work
orders as I can. Does that sum it up?"

Andy grinned, happy with the new hire. "You got it. This is
the last part of your rounds down here. You just have to walk
through the basement and make sure all the pumps are working."

Peter nodded and followed the bald, portly old man. Although he had only met Andy at the beginning of the shift, the
man had already irritated Peter. This irritation always arose
when circumstances forced Peter to be around another human
for too long.

After allowing the heavy metal door to the basement to slam

shut behind him, Peter turned his cautious gaze down the dimly lit staircase. A sudden chill ran up his spine, and the sensation of being surveilled brought the hairs on his skin to attention; every inch of his body grew alert.

"This is my least favorite part of the night." Andy cleared his throat. "I hate going down here. Gives me the creeps."

"Why is it so different down here compared to the rest of the building?" Peter tried to shake the eerie ambiance he felt. The architecture of this sublevel seemed so old compared to the rest of the structure; an arcane décor had taken over.

"This building has been here for almost two hundred years, give or take — built way back when." Andy continued.

"What year?" Peter's curiosity took hold.

"Around 1810. Could have been before or after, but you get the idea. This part of the basement is the oldest. Over time, the rest of the facility grew around the original." Andy sighed, wanting to escape the creepy sensations looming in the air. "Let's keep moving. We've got five pumps to go over."

Peter followed Andy down the staircase, where the amount of lighting did little to brighten up the dark feelings. A long corridor met them at the bottom of the stairs. With careful haste, Andy instructed Peter on the remaining aspects of completing the nightly rounds. He led Peter through the intersecting corridors to long basement tunnels and unlocked boiler rooms to inspect the tucked-away equipment. With each step taken, Peter became more than confident that something — not someone — monitored his every move.

SIXTH NIGHT

After five days of constant instruction, Peter worked his first night shift alone. Relief filled his soul. The freedom to ponder, alone, and be at peace without the outside distraction of others soothed his anxiety-ridden soul. This type of solitude made Peter feel at home.

Upon completing the first set of rounds, which included Peter checking the first and second floors, he stumbled upon work orders strewn about in a careless pile on the communal workbench. The second shift always vacated in a hurry. One work order stuck out for reasons beyond Peter's understanding. He lifted the piece of paper, reading the printed text.

REQUESTOR'S NAME AND POSITION:
Andy, Maintenance Engineer Level II

DATE:
February 12, 2008

REQUEST:
Take insect spray and spray all the corners and walls in the primary basement corridor. Laundry transport staff spotted ants.

LOCATION:
Basement. Primary corridor.

Peter remembered the eerie atmosphere pressing down on him, and the paranoia of being monitored inside the basement returned. The sudden fear chilled him to the bones.

It's just a basement, Peter thought.

* * * *

The silence blanketed Peter as he descended the cement staircase. The sensation of unseen eyes intensified; the hairs on his body stood from head to toe. Each step seemed louder than it should have been as his foot touched the damp corridor ground. He tried slowing his pace to control and soften the landing of his boots to cement; it did little good.

As he reached the middle of the corridor, he caught a small army of red ants moving back and forth as if on a mission of the utmost importance. What struck Peter as strange was that they didn't gather food as ants are wont to do. The tiny creatures appeared to be waiting for him, and Peter swore their movements stopped one after another like a wave of dominos. All activity ceased, and the ants stood before Peter, looking in his direction.

What the fuck is this?!

With a deep sigh, Peter took a few more steps toward the small red blotch of ants. The lighting cast a slight glow as he approached them, and he held the spray that would terminate the vile creatures. A maddening flash of jumbled imagery shot through Peter's mind at that moment. He dropped the spray gun and cradled his head in pain.

What's happening to me?

The imagery soon became apparent after a few heartbeats of pain and confusion. Peter held the image of a woman in his mind. She was a beautiful woman with soft white skin and hair as red as his own. She smiled at him with a posture demanding he come closer. An uncontrollable, animalistic lust took control of his body.

Jesus Christ! What's happening to me?!

The lust intensified as imagery of the naked woman with flowing red hair continued to flash through his mind. Her curves were beyond sensual, and her smile became more seductive than any physical touch.

It dawned on Peter that the army of red ants surrounded him, and the ants were broadcasting the imagery and sensations.

"What do you want?!" Peter yelled in a fit of furious anger.

He did his best to break his mind free of the images. The more he tried to sever the connection, the more insatiable the lust grew.

Why is this happening?

While falling to his knees, the ants approached as if welcoming one of their own. A distinct scratching noise originated from behind the wall to Peter's left. He studied the wall in utter horror as the bricks tumbled out of place with some force and rattled on the damp cement floor. The head of an ant, the size of a small dog, poked out and peered in Peter's direction.

Try as he might, Peter could not make a sound to match the petrified fear on his pale face. The last image Peter beheld before blacking out was that of many giant ants emerging from the hole in the wall and heading straight toward him.

* * * *

He awoke in a room that had been void of human presence for a long time; the light illuminated little. Peter stood up, discovering his nakedness, and studied his prison with a curiosity that blanketed the fear. The sound of the giant ants marching across the cold cement ground caught his attention, and his eyes focused on the open doorway with renewed horror.

What are these things?

We are of the same origin, Peter. A female voice spoke in his mind. *Follow the children to me.*

Two giant ants stood by the doorway, facing Peter. Unsure of what to do, Peter obeyed the voice, taking careful steps with his bare feet to navigate the cold, uneven cement floor. The two giant ants led him down a series of strange subterranean corridors that were like those of the facility but untouched by anyone in ages.

Two ant guards led Peter to another opening in the wall of one corridor. The organic membrane of a new passage shocked and awed Peter simultaneously. The membrane was flesh-toned, and Peter peered through it to glimpse other ants walking about.

Enter. The female prompted within his mind.

Peter entered the strange tunnel of organic membrane and experienced the warmth of the fleshy substance upon the souls of his bare feet. He disregarded the sensation and continued walking as naked as the day he was born. The two giant ants stayed behind at the entrance of the strange subterranean dwelling, and Peter continued, unsure of what he would find next.

At the end of the corridor was an open area. The walls comprised the same substance as the tunnel. In an odd way, the immense room invited Peter like a long-lost lover, and he drowned in a strange sense of belonging.

I've been waiting a long time for you, Peter. I lost you long ago. You were born to serve. That is why you have returned to me. The female voice seemed stronger in his mind.

"Where are you?" he asked, praying he wasn't going crazy.

The membrane opening and separating startled Peter; a gelatinous substance fell off the open edges with a sticky splat that disgusted him. Emerging from the opening was the beautiful woman who appeared in his visions. Her stance was seductive, and Peter was powerless against the woman. Her curves were as sensual as he had seen within his visions. The sudden lust took over, and his nakedness did nothing to hide the sudden erection.

Sensing his unease, she took a comforting step forward. "It's okay. This is where you belong."

"I don't understand." Confusion filled the young man.

The redheaded woman caressed Peter's face. Her touch soothed the senses as she closed her eyes. Flashes of imagery bombarded Peter; they revealed his true origins, and it turned out that he wasn't human after all. He was born of the colony to one day be called upon to serve and reproduce. He was a stud, and the human form masked his true nature. He was a creature like the ants and the woman standing before him.

"Who are you?" Peter asked, drunk with the new knowledge that flooded his senses.

She kissed him on his forehead with a gentle smile. "I am your Queen."

The kiss was beyond perfection, and the ecstasy of being near her soft, smooth skin was maddening. Peter gave in to the lust and allowed her to take control. He was soon on his back, and she mounted him with majestic dominance. The two made love on a level that was beyond anything he had ever experienced. Life and death were irrelevant. The moment was overpowering. He transcended into something more and connected to the colony. He was a part of them. He fit in.

The climax left his body trembling; he opened his euphoric eyes; her enticing smile greeted him. It brought Peter boundless joy to please his queen. What distressed Peter next was that the image of a beautiful woman changed. Her features transformed from a human into something else; a hybrid insect revealed itself, and Peter witnessed with petrified horror as the inhuman creature continued to straddle his naked body.

His own flesh rippled, changing shape and shade. A silent gasp escaped his changing mouth; antlike mandibles protruded, and his speaking ability vanished. The human shell he and others had seen for so long melted away. He became what he was meant to be.

It's okay, Peter. You did well. She reassured with the confidence of a lover.

Peter experienced a sense of ease coming from the voice. He had served his purpose. His seed would help breed a new colony, and his kind would live on. A sense of peace and happiness took hold as his flesh was being eaten, first by the queen and then by the giant ants that lived beneath the facility. It comforted Peter that he wasn't alone; finally, he fit in.

LOST AT SEA

STORY 7

August 5, 1885

MY CLOSEST COMPANION of countless years has perished and moved on from this plane of existence; it bereaves the better sensibilities from my body, leaving only the soulless shell of a man. The numbing emptiness remaining is nothing more than a reminder of how I am responsible for Nolan's demise. Blood is on my hands; they are the hands of an enemy, for no longer can I view the friendship of old in good repute.

I never intended for Nolan's death. Across the vast ocean, Kingstown awaited the both of us. I stored the relic with assiduous attentiveness; it sits now in my possession. The seax is of significant value to those who understand the scramasax for its true nature. The elder blade is more than a mere instrument of destruction. This artifact is also a key to a long-forgotten container. The contents of this container remain an elusive mystery, though the scroll unearthed by Nolan hints at treasures of inestimable wealth long forgotten.

The day Nolan discovered the scroll existed was an excitable turning point; the world changed for my lifelong friend and would never again be the same. I'd never seen Nolan so invigorated with the sense of wonder we both thought lost to childhood. His typical demure nature was so overcome with a determined fanaticism that I, at one point, thought an institution for those with mental ailments would be the only acceptable remedy to calm the man. He composed himself from the antics of the escaped child, and Nolan explained to me how he came by such a scroll.

"Belg, my good man. You must understand my work is not the misguided fabrication of hopefulness but the result of extensive research." His enthusiastic voice sounded earnest beyond reckoning. The child was on the verge of escaping the man once again.

"Have a seat, old friend," I gestured for Nolan to find comfort in a cushioned chair in my study. I prepared a pipe to smoke and offered the customary beverage selection, which Nolan declined. As I reclined my body and relaxed with the lit pipe, I scrutinized Nolan with curious eyes. "What is it you believe you have found, Nolan? You speak as if you've made an amazing discovery."

I remember how he took his time. With painstaking care, he thought out each word within his fast-paced mind. After a moment of composure, he relaxed in his chair. "I have discovered a scroll, Belg. It leads to wondrous hidden treasures."

"I have treasure enough here in Wales." I gave him a polite smile while taking in the tobacco from my pipe. "Profits are exceptional, investments yield fantastic returns, and my purse gets fatter by the day."

I had never beheld such a disappointed expression on my

childhood companion's face before. I destroyed all he worked toward with a simple lack of enthusiasm. His dependency on my reaction disappointed me to the point of near outrage. How dare he put such expectations on our friendship? Of course, my ignorance regarding the validity of Nolan's claim was strong at the time.

"The last thing I wish to do is trouble you, Belg. I realize how successful you've become." His words struck a nerve, but I settled the guilt in the back of my mind and listened. "You are a wealthy man with gentlemanly means. You have a knack for business I never possessed, and therefore, it comes as no surprise we find ourselves here; you are the pragmatic realist, and I am the dreamer searching for glorious discoveries. I only wished to rekindle a sense of wonder we shared as boys and perhaps make true for ourselves an adventure we have only dreamed of."

The emotions within my logical mind came undone after those words touched my heart. Nolan was my childhood friend. We grew up together as brothers, and life gave us two distinctly different paths when those children matured into men. His parents fell ill, and mine prospered. Nolan worked to keep things afloat while I lived a more lavish lifestyle of comfort.

"Nolan. Tell me more. I wish to learn all about it." I took another puff off my pipe and settled into my chair.

"Of course, Belg. Of course." Nolan's enthusiasm returned, and as he explained the scroll to me, I grew enthralled with the greatness of it all. He rolled out the deteriorating parchment, presenting the cryptic nature of the information, and spoke of a unique blade. He believed he had uncovered the location of this scramasax and needed my help with safe passage. My company owned the quarry where this elder blade was buried.

The sea wind is cold, and I have a clear view of the setting sun. It will still be a while before we reach Kingstown. Once I arrive, I seek to uncover the treasure. Then and only then shall I learn if the sacrifice of my friend's life was worth it. As I retire for the night, I am disgusted that it just might be.

August 6, 1885

I awoke this morning to frantic deckhands bellowing outrage; a lifeless body lay out in the open, discovered by fellow crewmembers. No one aboard can explain the sudden death of what appeared to be a healthy and vibrant young man. His ghostly pale skin and eyes appeared drained of all essence.

A curse comes to mind. Nolan spoke of such things before he died, but I must remain calm and determined. This journey must be finished.

August 7, 1885

Paranoia has usurped the Captain's better sensibilities. He eyes the few passengers and crew onboard his ship with cold suspicion. Another crewmember is dead with no cause or explanation. Quarters are being searched for foul play. I can only hope the contents of my room remain elusive to the investigation and appear as the relics of an eccentric, wealthy gentleman.

Fear is in the air, mixed in with the salt of the sea, and gives off the most unsettling aroma. I discern it in the crewmen's eyes. It lives in the Captain's eyes. He is afraid but would never give credence to such fear. He must remain strong for his crew. I, too, am afraid. I fear this ship will never reach port in Kingstown. I fear I am a fool to believe such a thing to be possible.

As I gaze upon the endless blue of the open sea, I only think of Nolan and our last moments together. His wordless, deep blue eyes screamed at my betrayal of him. Do I deserve to be forgiven? His life ended because of my greed and instinct to survive. Did he deserve to die? His eyes grew as fierce and hungry as mine. The blade pulled this deep-rooted part of human nature from both of us. The damn thing is cursed, after all.

We'd still been in Wales. The night air was filled with wonder as we approached the particular quarry that granted me so much wealth. I sent the crew home, aware Nolan would desire complete privacy for our excavation. I drove the carriage myself, wanting to keep the entire adventure between two old friends, and as we approached the quarry, the comfort of the night air transformed into something else. A gloom hung over the mine, thick and uncomfortable.

"It's nothing to worry about, Belg." Nolan laughed off my feelings of disquiet. I knew he felt the same, but he pushed on, putting on a brave show. "Shall we have a look? You have a remarkable crew at your disposal. They've completed most of the digging for us, if not all of it."

"Would it not be advisable to proceed with caution?" I stepped down from the carriage and stood alongside my friend. "Mines can be dangerous to navigate."

"Have faith, Belg. The risk is well worth the benefits." Nolan assured me.

"If you might humor me, Nolan, there is a question I wish to ask. How did you conclude that the quarry under my company's name has the item you require within its belly?"

Nolan began walking toward the adit, eager to gain entrance. "The scroll I presented to you was written with a particular quill. I neglected to bring it with me when I visited your home to inquire about your willingness in this endeavor, but the quill has a unique design on the feather. That, combined with the cryptic nature of the scroll, allowed me to understand and determine I had the cipher needed to unlock the mysteries hidden within the scroll. I used the design on the feather of the quill. That design was no accident, Belg, for it allowed me to translate this location. When I discovered it was a quarry owned by you, it became clear this was providence."

We arrived at the vertical shaft and descended to the depths of the mine. The lighting was minimal. The cramped space with which to move about gave me a bout of manic claustrophobia, but I pressed on with the aid of Nolan. The digging was the most troublesome part. Nolan dressed for the occasion, and his impoverished upbringing accustomed him to manual labor. On the other hand, I was not, and I felt the strain and fatigue of what the mining crews dealt with daily.

The scramasax lit the belly of the mine once we unearthed it. The blade's glint made it appear alive. It drew our eyes in like a lover, and its power over us came with a suddenness neither of us could deny. The fatigue and tiredness of the endless digging faded away.

That's when the change took place. Nolan's greed and my own were on equal footing. He wanted the elder blade as much as I did. I had no choice but to acquire the blade for myself. We unearthed my property, which belonged to me; my right to it was indisputable. Nolan failed to grasp this.

"Belg, you may not have it!" His eyes were furious as he lunged for the blade. "It belongs to me, not you!"

I remember lunging toward the blade as well. My body did not feel like it was my own during those moments. A violent struggle ensued. I forget much of it now, but I remember that when it ended, I stood over Nolan's body, and the blade had shed a fair amount of his blood.

"It's cursed..." Nolan spoke his last words, spitting up bubbles of slick crimson. His body gave one last violent convulsive spasm and ceased to be a thing filled with life.

I stood for a few moments, unable to move. The fear and shock of what I had done paralyzed me. I write this out hoping to find meaning but am left riddled with guilt and remorse. In the blink of an eye, I murdered my best friend.

I exited the mine in a surreal state. I forced its collapse, doing my best to create the specifics of an accident. This allowed me to bury my wrongdoing forever. I promptly closed all operations the following day, stating I wished to move locations. My company's land was vast, and setting up another nearby quarry without ever having to uncover his body was simple.

One night, I sat in my study, enchanted by the blade's properties. It lay beside Nolan's notes of what this relic could unlock if taken to Kingstown. A deep desire to uncover this hidden wealth overwhelmed all else. I wanted the treasure, but I also owed it to Nolan, even if I had been the reason for his death.

August 13, 1885

A few of us have survived so far, and the Captain is dead. A carnal mutiny swept over the crew, and in my soul, I realized this was where I would die. A strange madness has overtaken almost everyone. A few passengers and crewmembers who maintained some semblance of sanity have banded together. We are secure in the lower deck, attempting to ascertain the next best course of action. As I study all their faces, I realize what is to blame. The elder blade in my possession is the culprit.

The crew and remaining passengers are nervous and quiet. We are trapped by the madness that gripped the others. A woman whose husband sent for her sat in a corner; her name was Annabelle. A lovely name. Her once elegant dress clung to her in ripped tatters; blood stains from the sudden violence that engulfed her like a storm glinted in the lamplight. The flummadiddle skirting the lower part of her dress frayed in uneven patterns.

"Are you well?" I cleared my throat, sure that my attempt at causerie was awkward given the circumstances.

She shook her head.

"Silly question." I offered my handkerchief. She dried her tears. I noticed a ring on her left hand. "Your husband awaits you in Kingstown?"

She nodded. "Yes. I return to him after visiting my mother." She dabbed at the silent tears with the handkerchief. "Machynlleth is where I am from. My father owns a small inn, and I must admit, they meet my arrival with pomp whenever I return home. A visitor to their fair countryside always elicits such excitable reactions."

"Warranted, I am certain." I smiled. It relieved me to see her smile in return.

Her eyes drifted in memory. "The town has that peculiar coloring I remember being struck with when I passed through it in childhood. I attended the Welsh morning service before my departure. It was such a thin congregation. I..." She locked eyes with me. Desperation sprang from them. "My husband, God bless his soul, never made much time for church. Are you a man of faith?"

I was taken aback by such questioning, although I shouldn't have been surprised. Life and death situations made one think of such things. I clutched the artifact closer to me. It rested on my lap in a sack. I scarcely had time to grab it before the horror of the mutiny ensued. Somehow, I also managed to bring my pipe, the rest of my tobacco, and some matches.

She noted my change in posture. Her eyes fell on the sack. "What is it you hold so dear?"

"Nothing!" I barked louder than intended.

The outburst caused the remaining survivors and crew to stare in bewilderment. Most of the men kept the door to the lower deck barricaded and guarded. The constant smashing against the defenses became melodic; the madness drove those intending us harm boundless stamina. They persisted without end.

"I... I apologize." I bowed my head, embarrassed, and left Annabelle to be. She would never see her husband again.

I paraded past the other survivors, holding the blade close. An unnatural fear that they might try to steal it from me bombarded my every thought. It was maddening. An infant cried, taking me away from thoughts of murder in the name of protecting this ancient seax whose thirst for blood knew no bounds.

The infant's cries drowned out the fearful murmurs and rang in unison with the constant banging against the barricaded door.

The combined noises were a macabre melody syncing in harmonies created by a devilish composer.

"Shut that child up!" cried a deckhand, a young blond man. It was his first voyage and would be his last.

"Shut yourself!" The father barked in return, with violence in his eyes.

The blade. The blade's need for bloodlust began to hold sway to those few who held out this long. I knew I had to act.

"Young man," I walked to the deckhand, who vainly ignored the crying infant. He could not deny the veracity of the cries.

"What ya' want?" His lowborn accent shone through. He cast aside formalities at this point. I couldn't blame him.

"What's the cargo down here? There appears to be more than mere passenger luggage." I studied the crates and barrels lined up and secured throughout the lower deck with militaristic precision.

"Gunpowder and a consignment of explosives are taking up the bulk. It was a last-minute addition to the cargo manifest. The Captain is..." He froze for a moment, remembering the dire situation. "That is, he was a man who liked to make the most of these trips. He always saw fit to make room for extra profit. It's what I was told, anyway."

It was then I realized I had two choices. I could allow the evil instrument to change everyone below deck, which it would. Violent, gruesome deaths would ensue, all by one another's hand. Or I could make it so this ship never reached port. We would drown at sea. This would be a mercy for those who survived this long, for it is better than killing your loved ones and dying a murderer — like me.

The blade had to vanish; it was far too dangerous. So, I write my final words, smoke my last bit of tobacco in my pipe, and plan to ignite the volatile contents of the lower deck pointed out to me by the young blond man. I never did ask him his name. There is enough explosive material here to ensure this ship sinks; with it, so shall the wretched blade. The ocean will have its offering on this day.

I store this journal within a bottle in hopes it remains and may one day be discovered so the truth can be revealed. I've placed it on the opposite end of the lower deck, away from where the explosion will happen. I leave my signature with this journal and hope it will be treated as a last will and testament if found. My wealth, if any should remain, is to go to Nolan's family. He was survived by a sister, nephews, and nieces. They deserve a better life. May all onboard this ship forgive me. May Nolan's family forgive me, and may this cursed artifact never be discovered again.

SHIFTING REALITIES

STORY 8

I COULDN'T REMEMBER anything when I awoke in the middle of the woods in western Michigan. Still, somehow, I knew Michigan was where someone or something deposited my body. I was alive. I had that going for me.

The Manistee National Forest engulfed me. Flashes of foreign imagery broke through the silence of my mind as I attempted in vain to find out why I woke up naked in the middle of the woods. At that point, I couldn't recall my name. I knew it was cold; the weather was unforgivingly cold to a naked man. Winter was on the horizon. I could feel that much as I got my bearings while surrounded by conifer and hardwood trees; the forest spread on rolling hills as far as my eyes could see, packed dense with nature. My stomach gurgled; the sound surprised me. The sensation was hunger. Whatever incident it was that took place to leave me in this state also left me with little energy, so my survival instincts took complete control. Shelter, food, and water.

These were the only things on my mind.

Standing upright challenged my body. My body felt like it hadn't been used in ages, and it fought me as I did my best to command it to move as I wanted. I told myself to walk, but there were misfires. It was like walking wasn't what I was used to. My physical form screamed for me to crawl on all fours. It didn't make a hell of a lot of sense to me, but it would later. By this point, my eyes were fully adjusted, and I took a moment to study my surroundings. I couldn't distinguish any visible trails, and the earth's dirt appeared undisturbed, save for animal tracks. My instincts told me this area wasn't foreign to people, and since my instincts were all I had, I let them guide me. I began trudging barefoot and naked through the cold forest in the direction that simply *felt* right.

I walked for about an hour; for reasons beyond me, I stopped. I *felt* like I had to. Beyond that, I had no valid reason to cease my wandering. Weary and tired of trudging through the forest, I sat on a log, feeling uncomfortable. I didn't care that the flesh of my rear rested upon the rough surface. I was shrouded in nothing but trees, and there was still no sign of a trail. A bald eagle sounded overhead, mocking the lone human out of his element. A white-tailed deer sprang from the brush, ignoring me as it went about its business.

I was lost and confused. I fought to remember anything. Why couldn't I recollect my identity? The sound and sensation of my stomach rumbling overpowered those thoughts. A forceful and abrupt hunger pang squeezed my insides, making me want to sicken up. I held my stomach in famished pain and heard a rustle from the trees surrounding me.

"Hello?" I surveyed the area for signs of another person. I sensed something or someone near me, but I couldn't pinpoint the exact location.

The rustling of branches and trees was faint yet sounded closer. Whatever was out there wouldn't show itself, making me nervous. I forgot the hunger. Adrenaline pumped through my system as the fight-or-flight response kicked in. The creature was upon me.

The roar of the black bear startled me beyond words, and I remained seated, petrified with fright. As I turned, I was astonished because I didn't feel this incredible creature move near me at all, and as it roared, standing on its hind legs, I fell backward off the log. My head landed hard on a branch, and the darkness enveloped me, taking me from the frightful situation.

* * * *

My eyes opened to what appeared to be a ceiling of dirt carved into the earth, with wooden beams acting as some kind of support system. The blanket covering my body warmed my flesh and remained inviting, and I realized I was now fully clothed. The alluring aroma of a stew invaded my nostrils, and my stomach rumbled with the fury of a mighty beast. As I sat up with slow, deliberate movements, I discovered a man near a cauldron of sorts preparing the food responsible for the mouthwatering aroma.

"It's about damn time you woke up. You've been out for quite a while. Do you mind telling me just how the hell you ended up naked in the middle of the woods?" The man's eccentric gaze remained on the food he prepared, and he sat on a small bench near the cauldron.

"To be perfectly honest, I can't remember anything," I replied.

The man grunted as if it were just his luck. He didn't act the least bit surprised. "Are you telling me you can't remember anything at all?"

I nodded. "I'm afraid so. Where did the bear come from?"

"I'm more concerned about your origins, friend." The man took the oversized wooden spoon he used to stir the stew and poured the mouthwatering dish into a bowl. He brought it to me and placed it in my hands, saying, "My name is Sylvester. Yeah.

That sounds good. You can call me Sylvester."

"Pleasure to me you. Thanks for helping me and for the clothes." I began eating the stew, disregarding how hot it was. I tolerated the heat of the meal, knowing full well my body demanded nourishment.

"You're mighty welcome there, friend." He smirked at me and began studying my face with a quizzical intensity. It made me uncomfortable as I ate.

"What is it?" I asked between stuffing my mouth with heaping spoonfuls of savory stew.

"I just noticed that you have a nice minor bump there on your cheek. It looks like a pimple. It's big too. Say, you ever watch television? I occasionally do. I don't own one myself, but it reminds me of a certain television show I viewed once upon a time. Mind you, this was before all that streaming became all the rage with people." He cracked his neck as he explained.

"What are you talking about?" I asked, confused by the conversation. Being attacked by a black bear was strange enough, but talking about television to a stranger who put clothes on my naked body while I was unconscious took it a step further.

"I'm talking about that there hypnotic zit you got on your cheek there. Say, you don't remember your name at all, do you, friend?" He inquired again.

I shook my head from side to side as I continued to eat.

"Well, I can't keep calling you friend, so in honor of that mark on your face there, I'm going to call you Pastulio. Named after that character on a television show I saw." He smiled, revealing perfect teeth. Being an outdoorsman must have provided an excellent dental plan.

Words couldn't describe how dumbfounded I became. I had a hard time believing events were unfolding in this manner.

The stranger nodded again. "Yup. Pastulio it is. Nice to meet you, Pastulio."

"Are you serious?" My left eyebrow rose. I didn't even know I could do that.

"Always am." Sylvester stood from the side of my bed and

filled a bowl of savory stew for himself. Sitting near the cauldron, he ate slowly, enjoying each bite as if it were a delicacy.

At that moment, a potent image flashed through my mind. I was certain a lost memory had resurfaced. I experienced traveling through the woods. I was looking for something. What was I looking for? The name of a town came to mind. Arcadia. Somehow, I learned of the optical illusion. It was the place everyone called gravity hill or magnetic hill. The directions came back to me. If you take Highway M22 north, leading out of Arcadia for a few miles, you'll end up at Joyfield Road. The thing is, you don't stop there. You keep going a few more miles until you reach Blaine Church. I was there. I turned right at the church as instructed and ended up at the bottom of the hill a few hundred yards down.

"Putney Road..." I spoke to no one in particular.

"Come again?" Sylvester asked, now on his second bowl of stew.

I shot a glance his way, soaking in the curious expression on the face of the man who rescued me from my nakedness and the wilderness. And a black bear, come to think of it. I don't think the eagle and white-tailed deer represented a threat.

"You mentioned Putney Road." He said.

I nodded. "Yes. I was there. I remember leaving Arcadia and heading to the hill. I was at gravity hill. I don't remember why, though."

"Gravity hill? That's where cars roll uphill. The magnetic fields are all wonky, according to some. Some even hazard supernatural work is at play. Most people just chalk it up to an optical illusion these days." Sylvester nodded, understanding. "Do you remember what happened once you got to the hill?"

Pieces came back to me. "It was the illusion. I wanted to see it. I *felt* I needed to see it. It's like it was calling me."

"That sounds mighty interesting there, my friend." Sylvester ate more of his stew.

"Where are we now?" I asked.

"Right now, we're in my home. It was built a long time ago.

It's kind of a starting point." Sylvester admitted.

"What do you mean?" I removed the rest of the blanket from my body and set the bowl of food down near a small wooden nightstand. As I panned the entire area, I discovered all the furnishings were made of wood, and an odd variety of items were strewn about as if they had been collected over a very long time.

"Do you like cupcakes?" Sylvester stood from where he sat near the cauldron and moved to grab a bag. He removed a few packaged cupcakes you could find in just about any vending machine.

"What?" The randomness of the conversation wasn't helping my lack of memory.

"Cupcakes, Pastulio, do you like them?" He asked again.

"I guess." I shrugged.

Sylvester tossed one in my direction as he opened his own and ate it. "I love these things."

"I appreciate the food." I stood up, eager to move on. I realized I had shoes on my feet. This man had given me socks and shoes. "But I need to keep moving."

"Where to?" He asked as he sat down near the cauldron again.

"I don't know. I just know that I need to keep moving." My eyes were desperate for answers.

"Which direction?" He asked, licking his fingers after the last bite of his dessert.

Without thinking, I turned and pointed to my left. Sylvester's face beamed with the biggest smile I'd ever seen. "What is it?"

"That's toward Rose City. There's another gravity hill there, my friend. Looks like you're tuned into them." His smile remained.

I fought against the mounting confusion. "But I don't understand why. And I don't understand why I can't remember anything else." I grew frustrated. A sense of claustrophobia smashed down on me. The room that was a sanctuary suddenly felt like a trap that I needed to free myself from.

"How far away am I?" I asked.

Sylvester cleared his throat. "Well, right now, we're still in the Manistee Forest. We have to be on the other side of the state."

The randomness of the items caught my attention again. I recognized a fondue pot collecting dust in a corner near a single flip-flop. Other trinkets were strewn about, like toy cars, old photographs, cameras from various periods, a musket, and even a toothbrush that I'm sure was much older than me.

Sylvester beamed with pride. "That's a nice collection there, huh, friend." He was making a statement.

"Do you even use this fondue pot? It's dusty as all hell. And who keeps a single flip-flop lying around?" I turned my attention back to Sylvester.

"I might just have one leg someday and not want to wear a regular shoe. And don't go judging me there, Pastulio. I collect what I find, and what I find can be useful at some point. You just never know." He finished another cupcake and wiped the crumbs from his mouth. "So, you really feel you need to get to that other gravity hill?"

I nodded.

"Then we better get a move on. It's been a while since I used a car, so you'll have to be patient with me while I get it to work. Just sit tight in the meantime." He stood, ready for action.

"You're going to help me?" I asked.

"Sure am. If you go out alone, you might get yourself all lost and naked again. Can't have that happen, Pastulio." Sylvester winked at me as he exited the shelter. He pulled aside a wooden door and walked up a few stairs into the sunlight. We had been beneath the surface of the earth in the forest.

So, there I was. I made a new friend whose true intentions I was unclear about, and we were about to take a road trip across the great state of Michigan. Go figure.

At that moment, I could feel the pimple Sylvester mentioned to me. I took hold of a hand mirror (one of the many items Sylvester collected) and studied my face. It was a nasty zit, all right.

Then, a funny thing happened. I focused on it going away, and a few seconds later, it disappeared. The sensation on my flesh was a strange tingling. In shock, I almost dropped the mirror but placed it back before clumsiness took complete control.

Did my skin just shift its shape? Transform?

* * * *

I didn't precisely remember car rides before my amnesia, but I can confidently say that this one was perhaps the longest of my life. The old beat-up red truck dotted with rust holes started the third time Sylvester tried to turn the engine. The lack of a muffler made the radio obsolete and thinking near impossible, but I attempted to figure out my predicament. I might have made some progress, but Sylvester's continuous rambling bombarded me; he managed to keep his voice louder than the booming engine. The man loved talking. I don't know if it had to do with the fact that he was alone and never got to speak to anyone or if he knew it was annoying the hell out of me. It was probably a bit of both.

The gravity hill of Rose City created the same sensations I experienced at the first one I encountered if my memory is to be believed. The impression of a force beyond ordinary understanding was strong and growing stronger. The force that called me had no physical means. It hung in the air the way a cloudy, damp day pulls you down. From visual cues alone, it appeared to be like any other road in any other state, but the optical illusion remained. But the optical illusion didn't make me want to be at gravity hill. It was the damn *feeling*. It felt like something called me and pulled me to this spot.

"We'll have to part ways soon here, friend." Sylvester smiled; he exited the rusty red truck and stepped on the road.

"What?" I didn't understand as I followed him out of the vehicle. What did he know that I didn't?

Sylvester leaned closer to me. "You're about to go on another trip, Pastulio. Don't worry, though. After this next one, you should be able to remember more of what's going on. It's been this way for a long time and with good reason."

I grew even more perplexed. My mind raced, and I felt a throbbing pain worsening within my head. The pulsating of my temples increased with intensity.

Sylvester patted my shoulder. "What you're feeling right now is how it goes. It happened to you at the first magnetic or gravity hill — whatever the hell the kids call it these days. These spots have been around for a while. Think of them as a gateway for our kind."

So many questions ran through my mind. It became difficult to pinpoint them all, and even more difficult to be angry at Sylvester for not being upfront with me about what he knew. The man understood far more than he shared with me when I awoke in his underground dwelling.

Sylvester gave me another pat on the shoulder. "Don't overthink it there, friend. Just go with it. That initial pain is energy forming. Your body isn't used to it yet, but it will be. It won't hurt to travel after this one, and it won't be this involuntary reaction you're going through, either. All your questions are going to be answered at the next stop. Trust me."

"Trust you? I don't even know you!" I fell to the ground in pain. The energy of the hill pulled at every inch of my body.

"Next stop, Canada. You'll be waking up somewhere in Quebec, if I remember right. Say hi for me when you see the others, friend." Sylvester grinned as he turned around and began walking back to his truck. The last thing I saw him do was open the driver's side door. Then there was darkness.

* * * *

A wave of relief rushed over my body as I awoke fully

clothed. At that point, I think the ordeal of having to trudge about naked again would have been too much to handle. It was still light outside, and I realized I was in a lush forest with the accompanying noises of the great outdoors in the background of my thoughts. Sylvester mentioned Canada before my sudden departure. Was I in Canada? How the hell did I get here? With wide eyes, I soaked in the forest's freshness, wondering how on earth I traveled this far north. The energy guiding me seemed to enjoy dumping me in forests.

My nostrils picked up on a specific scent. It wasn't exactly human, but close. How I could tell that much from the smell confused me because I wasn't exactly sure. I turned around and beheld *him* standing before me. Instead of a black bear on hind legs facing me, I encountered an enormous creature with a body covered in fur fit for his forest surroundings. How did I know it was a he? Let's just say the exposed male bits put that of every male human porn star to shame. The creature was naked, is what I'm getting at.

He stood about eight feet tall with a robust frame that made bodybuilders look weak. He had a prominent brow ridge and flat nose that amalgamates every simian creature scientists have cataloged. He towered over me, staring at me like a curious child who found a new toy. His dark eyes penetrated me as fear trickled throughout my entire nervous system, causing my body to twitch uncontrollably; I could only think of one thing to call him: Bigfoot.

He smiled. This threw me off. Right after, he shrunk in size. The phenomenon startled me as I studied him with curious amazement. The fur retracted, showing human skin, and the beast turned into a man no taller than me. He stood naked, yet unashamed, and continued to carry the same smile. He was an older man and appeared familiar. My memories fought to emerge.

"Hello. Son. It's been a while. Sorry I ran out on you when you were young, but that's how it goes for our kind. When the call comes, we have to follow it. There's just no way around that simple fact." The old man spoke up, maintaining a smile on his face. He eyed me up as if he had been expecting me.

"Son?" The confusion was maddening. "Do you know who I am? I haven't been able to remember anything for a while now."

"It happens this way." The naked old man reached down and picked up a backpack of sorts. His hair was graying but full — no sign of thinning. "I don't wander too far from my clothes when I want to change form."

I sighed. "I should be more shocked at what I just saw. But I'm not. Why is that?"

"That's because deep down inside, you know it's natural and the true reality of what I am and what you are." The old man slipped on a pair of jeans and followed that by putting on a shirt. The sinew of hard muscle popped through the clothing. He was very fit.

Another creature emerged from the forest. This Bigfoot was a female version. She trotted over and towered above the old man and me as we stood in the forest. Her height appeared to be around seven feet. Her robust frame still carried a feminine quality that made the sex stand out despite being covered in fur. Her form changed as well. The dark reddish fur adorning her body retracted, and her tan skin became more apparent. A naked woman stood before me; the dark brown hair on her head was the only hair left on her curvy body. She was beautiful and toned. I stared despite my best efforts not to. Most women don't stand in front of you naked. She didn't appear bothered by this and was comfortable with her nakedness, like the older man.

"Please excuse our new friend here. He's not used to our ways yet." The old man explained.

She giggled as she reached into the backpack. She couldn't have been much older than me as she kept her gaze in my direction while getting dressed. "I'm sure he'll catch on soon enough." She winked at me as she spoke the words.

"Are you going to explain things to me?" I fixed my eyes on the old man.

"I'll let your memories do the explaining." He reached out

and touched my forehead. The memories burst through like a battering ram against an inadequate door.

I recalled waking up in the forest in Michigan. I had been drawn to gravity hill. It was just too damn irresistible, and I was dumped in the forest after it transported me. I was scared, and my body felt strange. Then, I changed for the first time. I transformed and ripped the clothing from my body. Before I knew it, I was like the old man and the beautiful woman. I traversed the forest as a massive creature, taller than any man could dream to be. My body was covered in reddish-brown fur. My senses were sharper, my eyesight improved, and I could feel the forest in ways I never thought possible. No fear lived in me. It *felt* right. I explored everything, like a child experiencing life for the first time.

I ran into other animals along the way. The first was a black bear. It wasn't afraid. We sensed each other. There was an unspoken understanding. My body changed forms again. Before long, I transformed into a black bear. My body could shift shapes, and the perceptual experience of it awed me. Other creatures crossed my path. One by one, I changed into what they were and could move like them, seeing as they saw and feeling as they felt. I even flew. I was a bird who soared through the skies without hesitation or fear of falling. The transformations were many, and that's what led to my loss of memory. There were too many changes too quickly, and I lost my identity in the changing of forms. I woke up in human form, remembering nothing.

I returned my gaze to the old man, realizing a few other things. When I was a child, I had been adopted. My skin was tan. I grew up thinking I was Mexican. After a DNA test, I discovered I was Native American. I never knew my actual parents or where they came from. The system carted me around from home to home, and I never fit in anywhere; I was always the outsider. That was the old life. My new life unfolded in ways I never thought possible. When I studied the old man's features, I saw myself. I saw the face of my father.

Shaken by the flood of memories, I took a few steps back.

"So, you're my father? You're my real father?"

"Yes." The old man smiled. "The calling was strong soon after you were born. I wanted to stay, but no matter what I did, I kept ending up at gravity hill. I understood that the same thing would happen to you at some point. It's passed on in the blood."

"I thought those hills were just an optical illusion." My head spun with information. More unburied memories swam to the surface.

The old man put his arm through a strap on the backpack and let it rest on his shoulder. "Those gravity hills, as people call them, are ways of traveling for our kind. They've been around for a very long time, just as our people have been. And hiding an illusion as an illusion, well, it doesn't get much better than that."

"What are we?" I asked.

The woman spoke up after buttoning up her shirt. "We're shapeshifters. We're here and together, and every one of our kind always finds his or her way back home."

"Shapeshifters, huh? No wonder no one can ever find Bigfoot." I smirked and laughed to myself.

"I never did like that name." She walked over and reached her hand out for me to shake. "Welcome."

I took her hand and smiled in return. "So, we can change into any animal?"

"We sure can. We can also change into just about any creature you can imagine. It's literally the stuff of legends. Like we've been saying, our kind has been around for a long time." The old man walked closer to me. "Let me ask you something. Did anyone help you along the way?"

I nodded. "Yes. A guy by the name of Sylvester."

The old man laughed. "Since you couldn't remember who you were, did he give you a name after some television show, movie, or actor even? He does that. He knows you won't remember anything when he finds you. It's his way of having fun with the new ones."

I chuckled. "Yeah, he did. He gave me a name from a television show. And he says hi."

"We better get going." The beautiful woman with dark brown hair spoke. Her smile was extraordinary, and her voice comforting.

"I don't even know your names." I bounced my gaze between the two of them.

"Names don't matter anymore." The old man spoke up.

"What do I call you?" I asked, accepting that confusion would be a part of my life for a while.

"You'll catch on. It's part of our way." The woman walked back into the thicker part of the forest.

The old man smiled at me and placed a fatherly hand on my shoulder. "Son, I'm glad you made it after all this time."

I followed my father into the forest. I followed my father home.

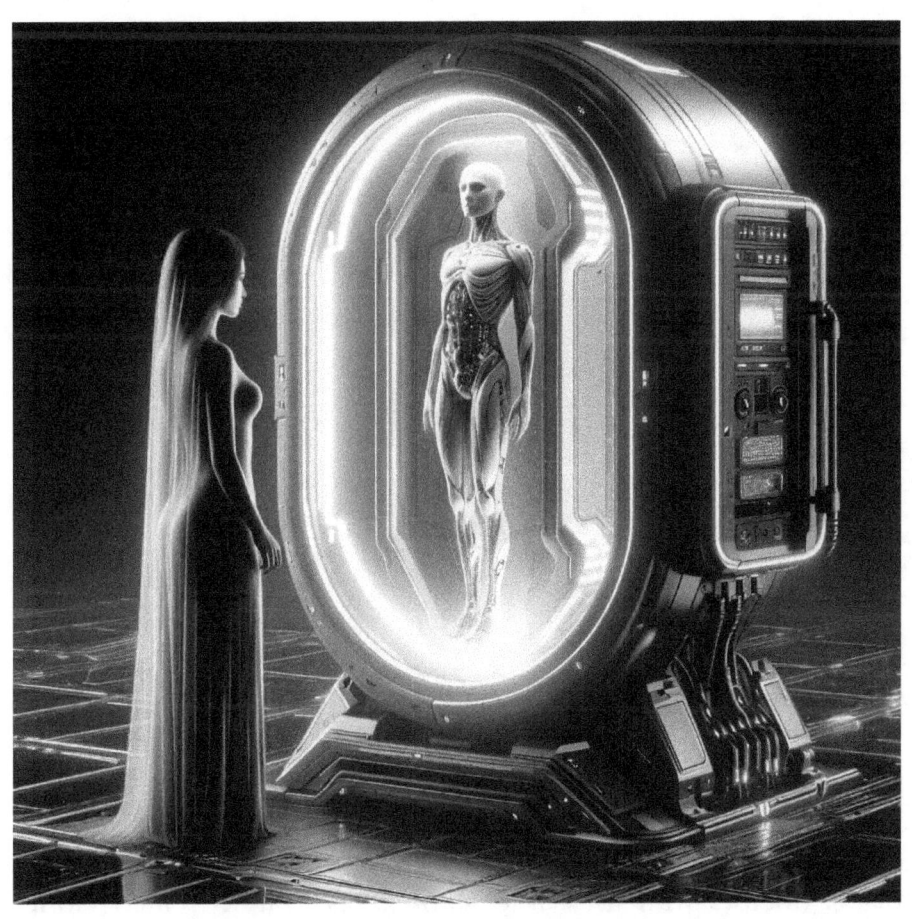

CLONING LOVE

STORY 9

"YOU ALLOWED THE notion of Rick's disappearance to prevail for the past six years as a missing person?!" The revelation shook Doctor Marek Potock to his core. It took the old man decades to climb out of the hole wrought with scandal encapsulating his early career. Before cloning became commonplace, doctors with the same leanings as Marek treated clones like true-born humans; Potock even facilitated the resurrection of loved ones to bereaved families. The shifting government policies and popular opinions on the subject led to the banning of cloning and the termination of all illegal clones.

"I needed to keep it a secret; people needed to believe he still lived. It was the only way I could have a chance at bringing him back." Ellen Crowberg, a woman approaching thirty, sat across from Potock in his office. She paid close attention to the doctor's expressions from the clinical chair made of uncomfortable plastic as Marek swiveled in his own chair behind the vintage desk.

Ellen's youth remained strong despite the hardships she faced. Her auburn hair clung to a vibrancy on the cusp of dimming. This contrasted with the much older Marek, whose hair abandoned the top of his head in a rush; the hair on the sides and back of his head refused to vacate, growing longer to compensate for the top's refusal to grow.

"What you ask of me is illegal. If caught, we'd face lifelong sentencing by the courts, at best, and at worst, execution. The government made their stance on cloning crystal clear." Doctor Potock's heavy eyes drifted off in deep thought. He served as Ellen and her late husband Rick's physician for the last decade, and it pained him to have her begging for such a request in his office.

"Please, Doctor Potock... Marek. You're the only one I can turn to. Believe me when I say I understand the consequences. I've been going over this in my head countless times, and the fact is, I am nothing without Rick. Please bring him back to me?" Ellen Crowberg did her best to maintain a sense of composure.

Marek cleared his throat and leaned forward with a consoling posture. "Dealing with previous memories can be hit or miss. Nothing about this can guarantee your Rick will be your Rick. He will have the same outside appearance and sound like him, but will he be him? I don't think so, Ellen. Too many clones have been unable to remember their previous life."

"No!!" Ellen shot up, unable to hold back her emotions. She paced the office, venting her anxious energy. "It's been six years! Six years of emptiness! In my heart, I'm certain this will work!"

With the ambulatory grace of a man in his last years, Marek stood from behind his desk and walked to Ellen. His expression beamed like a father talking down a child with genuine empathy. "Just because you wish it to be true does not make it so."

"This is all I have left, and you're the only one able to help me. Please?" Her eyes welled with tears. A slow trickle of them began as she fought to bottle the imminent eruption of pain and loss.

Ellen might as well have been Doctor Potock's flesh and blood. How does one turn down family? With a deep sigh, he stepped away and turned his back to her. "Do you have a sample?"

Ellen's eyes lit up. "I do." She wiped the tears away as hope took over.

Potock forced a smile to match Ellen's enthusiasm. "Bring it to me and be quick about it. I want to finish the procedure as quickly as time will allow."

* * * *

The advent of the regrowth module served as a crowning scientific achievement. The technology represented a harmonious integration of biology, nanotechnology, and artificial intelligence, allowing individuals to regenerate living organisms in a controlled and responsible manner within the confines of their personal laboratories. At first, the practice prospered. It was short-lived; it didn't take long for the government to commandeer the tech for its own purposes.

A lab needed to have a controlled environment to mimic the natural conditions required for the optimal growth of a human. This included maintaining specific temperatures, humidity, and atmospheric conditions to support cellular regeneration. The conditions in the underground lab remained less than ideal; the decaying equipment barely met the necessary standards.

They equipped the module with gel packs of nanobots on the verge of expiration. These nanobots carried sophisticated sensors and programmable functions; they also served as the foundation for initiating and guiding the regrowth process at the cellular level. High-speed DNA sequencers from older growth modules were attached to the makeshift lab, ready to analyze the genetic code from the sample of Ellen's late husband; the replication mechanism from a foreign module belonging to a nation where cloning remained legal sat ready to recreate an accurate genetic blueprint.

Marek moved on to inspect the biomechanical reservoir. The bioactive compounds, growth factors, and nutrients essential for cell development appeared optimal. These biochemicals would be dosed and released to promote optimal growth conditions. Another integral module component was the 3D bioprinting framework, which assembled complex structures by layering cells, tissues, and supporting materials.

Doctor Potock, now immersed in a scientific mindset, checked the environmental controls before a last inspection of the AI system. AI played a crucial role in orchestrating the cloning process. These algorithms would interpret the genetic data, monitor cellular development in real time, and adjust the parameters to ensure the clone's proper formation.

A considerable risk of being apprehended pushed Marek to work with speedy diligence. Doctor Potock had no choice but to accept the underground facility and hand-me-down equipment at his disposal. With a heavy sigh, Marek went to work.

Ellen waited twelve hours. What was twelve hours when compared to six years? Occasionally, she moved to use the restroom but, otherwise, remained glued to the procedure, knowing each passing minute brought her closer to Rick's return.

The growth module completed the process, speeding up the growth to make Rick the proper age. Ellen soaked in every detail of the massive contraption in utter amazement. Such creations remained illegal in most of the developed world; a few outliers stayed firm in their conviction of clone rights.

Potock sauntered over to Ellen with heavy eyes. A weary expression transformed into a delighted smile. "It was a success."

Tears streamed down her face. Seeing her beloved after six years released a joy she never thought herself capable of again. "Can I see him?"

"Not yet. He needs to rest. Jogging his memory may take some time. It might not happen at all. Regaining memory is hit or miss. We must review where Rick has been for the last six years. If he remembers nothing, all the better. Amnesia would explain why he hadn't attempted contact for so long. With his military background, it's not unusual for such things to occur with the nanotech injected into soldiers. I can help with medical backing to support this, along with some colleagues who share my ideas on cloning. We also need to go over other things, such as his paperwork. We need to ensure all his information is current and can withstand intense scrutiny." Marek sighed again. The weight of his age pressed down upon the old man.

"Doctor Potock. I... I need to." Disregarding the doctor's instructions, Ellen ran toward the end of the module.

A body identical to the man she loved with all her heart rested inside a module with a glass covering. She almost forgot his handsome appearance and savored his delicate features and short, black hair. The tears kept coming as she held her mouth to stop from whimpering.

Potock advanced with care; he became startled at the sudden aggressiveness of the hug Ellen gave him but relaxed as she let the strength of the embrace loosen. "It's okay Ellen. He's back. And no one will take him away again." Marek wished he believed the statement.

* * * *

Rick. Rick is supposed to be my name. The clone scrutinized the home the strange woman named Ellen brought him to. The house had a familiar spark, but he recalled nothing specific. He stood before a wall-mounted mirror used for last checks near the front doorway. He studied his own reflection. "I'm a clone?"

"Yes, and no. You're still Rick. My Rick." Ellen moved to embrace him and experienced a stabbing hurt in her chest when he took a step back. She took a deep breath, firm in her beliefs. "Your memories are going to come back to you."

"That's what you keep saying. But I remember nothing!" Rick

punched the mirror in a fit of rage; the glass cracked, and a few shards fell to the floor. His hand bled, and he stared at it in awe. This sensation of pain was new yet familiar.

"Rick!" Ellen moved to examine the hand. "Let me clean it up."

"No! Stay away!" A forceful shove sent Ellen backward, hitting the floor with a loud thud. "Who the hell am I supposed to be?! I don't remember! All these people you keep bringing here, I don't recognize them! I can talk, I can read, I can do all those things, and I'm not sure how that's possible because I'm a damn clone!"

With fearful eyes, she stood and straightened her dress. Ellen pushed back the urge to run and anchored herself using the love she carried for Rick. "Those are part of your memories. The other parts will come back to you." She walked to him with cautious steps and held the wounded hand.

"Ellen," Rick said her name with an apologetic tone. "Elly, please stop. I can do it myself."

Ellen froze. "What did you call me?"

Rick shrugged. "Elly. Why?"

Her face beamed with hope. "Only you called me Elly."

Still fearful of another outburst, Ellen moved more carefully to hold Rick; she grew desperate to wrap her arms around him. He did not step back, nor did he put up a fight. He hugged her back, confused and scared; to say he experienced an existential crisis, put it lightly.

I hope to God those memories come back. The clone thought.

* * * *

In a sudden and authoritative show of force, two government agents clad in black suits stormed into Marek's office, their demeanor radiating a palpable air of official urgency. Marek's office door swung open with a resolute thud, drawing the doctor's attention with immediacy. Their polished black shoes echoed with purpose on the tiled floor, and the sharp contrast of their dark attire against the sterile, clinical environment made them the focal point. Doctor Potock's assistant, Lily, trailed behind the imposing men, powerless to stop them.

"What is the meaning of this?!" Potock demanded.

"Doctor Marek Potock, my associate and I are here to discuss some of your recent medical activities not pertaining to this clinic." Agent Jones smirked as he sized up the good doctor. Jones stood tall and composed, exuding a silent authority most people bowed to on a subconscious level. His black sunglasses concealed any hint of emotion, adding to the mystery of his presence. The tailored suit accentuated a physique that hinted at discipline and strength despite the graying hair and aged facial features behind the glasses.

Lily's outrage made her tiny frame grow to intimidating heights if the anger had been directed at untrained civilians. "You can't come in here disturbing Doctor Potock like this! He has patients that need his full attention, and..."

"Lily, it's okay," Potock interjected. "I'll be speaking with these men in private."

"But..." Lily surrendered to Doctor Potock's command, whipping her blonde hair as she turned to the door; before exiting the office, she gave the agents one last disapproving glare.

Upon Lily's exit, Marek stood from behind his desk to meet them both at eye level. "Who are you, and what do you want?"

"We are with the Division of Illegal Cloning. I am Agent Jones, and this is Agent Li. And you are going to be placed under arrest for the illegal cloning of one Rick Crowberg, Doctor Potock." Jones answered.

How did they find out? Potock eyed the phone at his desk; vintage landlines came back in style to counter the era's digital dominance. A constant economic battle existed between analog and digital in the technological marketplace.

"Oh, Marek, you can try to warn Ellen, but it won't matter.

Our men are already en route, along with local authorities. They should be at her home any second now. The clone will be terminated, and Ellen will be arrested since I'm sure you aren't the sole architect of this deviant act against our laws." Jone's smile was chilling at best.

Agent Li moved toward Doctor Potock with a sense of controlled urgency. The taser-equipped handcuffs he carried underscored the gravity of the situation. These handcuffs would pulse currents of electrical charges should the detainee resist. Despite Agent Jones' and Li's shared attire, Li's demeanor presented a subtle contrast — a blend of vigilance and readiness. Dark eyes scanned the room with keen awareness, noting every detail.

"Ellen..." Potock whispered her name. *Forgive me for failing you.*

* * * *

After all that, she still wants to make me dinner. The clone let the thought go as he cleaned up the glass mess of the broken mirror. He couldn't help but study his reflection in each piece; the fractured image better represented his emotional state. *She'll be back soon.* The clone's mind remained on Ellen, who had stepped out to go shopping moments ago. *I can at least make the place look nice for her.*

The phone attached to the wall in the hall rang, taking Rick from his moment of introspection. Ellen voted with her dollar, and her vote went to analog tech; landlines had made a comeback. He answered and grew worried as Ellen's voice spewed fast, shaken words; fear enunciated every syllable. "Slow down. What's the matter?"

Ellen's warning created a primal panic in the clone. Yes, he was a clone, but he still wanted to live. "How did they find me?"

The question was one Ellen did not have an answer for, and Rick dropped the phone, exiting through the kitchen backdoor with the speed of hunted prey.

Upon exiting the house, two men dressed in black suits closed in on Rick, attempting to hold him down. The scuffle knocked over a patio table and pottery containing some of Ellen's favorite plants. Neighbors monitored the struggle with fascinated horror; a few recorded the incident on their cell phones only to have other agents nearby apprehend the devices with cold efficiency.

Much to Rick's surprise, he fought against his attackers using aggressive self-defense techniques; the origins of his martial prowess added to the mystery of his identity. Without thinking, he lifted a handgun from within the jacket of one of his attackers. It felt so natural.

How did I do that? The clone wondered.

Without wasting a second, Rick continued his run, leaving the two agents on the lawn of his home. His home?

I may have killed! The brief encounter ran through his mind as he sped away on foot. He recalled a snapping noise as he fought off one of the men. *Was that his neck?* The question horrified the clone.

In the quiet suburb, where trimmed lawns and white picket fences defined the landscape, Rick continued his run at a near superhuman pace, weaving through the labyrinth of residential streets. The tranquility of the surroundings clashed with the urgency of his footsteps as government agents closed in, determined to apprehend the clone.

The suburban streets bathed in the sun's warmth and didn't care about the fugitive clone. The peaceful neighborhood became an unexpected battleground. The quaint houses witnessed the unfolding drama; their windows framed curious onlookers peering out with a mix of concern and intrigue.

I have to escape! I have to live for Ellen!

Sirens broke his train of thought, warbling in the air. The fast-paced thud of airship blades overhead added to his already elevated heartbeat. Rick's footsteps echoed against the streets as he darted around corners. Picket fences and manicured lawns became an improvised obstacle course, each hurdle adding to the suspense of the chase. More sirens. More agents on foot. There was more yelling for him to stop. The rhythmic pounding of shoes from his escape reverberated in the clone's ears.

"He's over here!" A little boy shouted as police on foot did their best to maintain a solid pursuit. Excited by all the commotion, the boy jumped up and down, thinking the scenario to be an extravagant production created for him.

The clone of Rick did his best to ignore the boy. He cut through yard after yard, jumping fence after fence, unsure where to go. The thought of being caught motivated him to maintain a solid distance between himself and those pursuing.

In a desperate bid to evade capture, the clone reached the outskirts of the suburbs, where the asphalt gave way to the uneven terrain of a dense forest. The foliage loomed with an inviting yet ominous appeal, a refuge offering both concealment and uncertainty. With a final glance back at the agents closing in, the clone plunged into the forest, leaving behind the suburban streets.

The forest now played host to the frantic pursuit. Rick's clone navigated through the underbrush, the rustling leaves and animal sounds adding a layer of tension to his escape. The setting sun filtered through the dense canopy, casting dappled shadows on the forest floor. The airship pilots grew frustrated as their bird's-eye view became obsolete.

Rick disappeared deeper into the woods, and the government agents faced the challenge of navigating the unfamiliar terrain in suits and police uniforms. The chase unfolded beneath the overarching branches. As the benefit of the sun gave way to the shadows of the night, the agents and local police fell back, setting up a perimeter and utilizing modern technology to combat the darkness.

The time it took for the authorities to regroup gave Rick all the time he needed to make nature his refuge. This forest was vast, and he realized he possessed survival skills greater than the average person. For now, he would stay hidden.

* * * *

"Is he still in the cave?" Agson asked Bartly; they stood far away enough to monitor yet remain hidden. Their camouflage gear also aided in this respect. The clone ran fast and hard to find refuge and made a home deep in the woods near a cave system.

Bartly stayed focused on the cave. Being a clone himself, Bartly understood the fear and confusion going through the mind of the one they tracked. "Hasn't moved. He's smart. Has survival training."

"Doesn't surprise me," Agson said. He noted the rugged features of the man's face. Sometimes, Agson thought Bartly was carved of stone. It contrasted Agson's features, which were softer and full of life.

Both men were clean-shaven of all hair on their heads. It existed as their code and as a ritual for the rebel clones. Doing so represented cutting ties with all aspects of their previous lives.

"Think he remembers anything yet?" Bartly never took his eyes from the cave.

"He might. The Division of Illegal Cloning is on his ass, for sure. They discovered his birth faster than I thought they would. This means they want him in a bad way. He's special somehow." Agson struggled with what to do.

"What a bunch of DICs." Bartly spat out; it was one of three repetitive jokes the man told. The Division of Illegal Cloning was a bunch of DICs, a stand-in for dicks.

Agson didn't respond. The tired joke did not warrant a response after hearing it for what could easily have been the millionth time.

"We should make contact. If he's going to trust us, he needs to know he's not alone." Bartley suggested.

"It's still too soon. He wouldn't trust us walking up to him.

He's been on the run for five days. He's still got the scent of Division agents in his nostrils; he might confuse us for them. You've read his file. He's a killer. Military trained. We play it safe with him."

Bartly took offense to the comment, and Agson picked up on this. Bartly thought himself the most elite of the clones living in secrecy.

"So, what do you want to do?" Bartly asked.

Agson smiled. "We'll let him find us."

* * * *

Since his birth in the cloning module, flashes of everything he had experienced soared through Rick's mind. The cave system gave the clone multiple places to hide; he switched where he slept frequently, using the shelter of the caves. He escaped, for now. What about Ellen? What would he do next? What could he do?

Can't stay here for too long. Must keep moving. A handful of wild berries entered his mouth; the sweet and tart combination left a robust flavor on his tastebuds. Again, much to his surprise, Rick discovered his aptitude for survival to be formidable. The body remembered the previous life, but his mind did not.

A rattling noise disturbed his quiet dinner of sorts; he spread out tiny breakable branches and foliage along specific paths leading to the cave. Anyone walking those paths would step on the hidden branches, revealing their approach. Quick to action, he held tight to the gun he stole during his escape and took careful steps from within his sanctuary. Upon exiting, he found a note, and various leaves covered the ground leading to the note. Someone did a not-so-excellent job hiding their footsteps and wanted Rick to detect it.

After checking the small perimeter, Rick's clone lifted the note. He sensed eyes on him from afar. Relax. Whoever is hiding out there would have moved in if they wanted that kind of confrontation.

The note read: We are like you. You have valuable skills that can help us; we need not tell you how to find us. Come to us. Join us. Find purpose and safety with your own kind.

Rick panned the trees surrounding his forest home. He searched for any signs of those monitoring him and found none.

* * * *

Ellen understood all prospects for a happy future died the moment they discovered Rick's clone. Her life was over, and the government would make sure of it. The Division of Illegal Cloning showed no mercy. There would be no leniency, even for those who cooperated in the capture of others. But she would betray no one and feared her long-time family friend, Doctor Potock, was already in custody and in a much grimmer situation than she was.

The door to her damp cell opened, and the corridor light trickled in. A man dressed in a black suit entered with an all-knowing smile. "Mrs. Crowberg, I'm sure I don't have to tell you how much trouble you're in. Or the kind of trouble." This agent carried ancient features; he stood as a relic from before the advent of cloning. His bald head reflected some of the light, and his nose drooped with age; sporadic liver spots dotted his skin.

"I did what I did out of love." Ellen did her best to stay strong. Rick showed her how - the real Rick.

"Your husband, when alive, served as a decorated military officer. His death was a tragedy, but he died with honor, doing his duty for God and country." The man in the black suit seated himself across from Ellen at the stainless-steel table; it was the go-to decor for the various detention centers the Division had at their disposal. The older agent's chair was of a more comfortable design and placed in the interrogation room for his convenience.

"A genuine tragedy. You should have mourned and moved on. Not bring him back. Why? Why go through all this trouble knowing it would be impossible not to get caught?"

"What are you talking about?" A disgusting knot of dread formed within Ellen's stomach.

"Come on, Mrs. Crowberg! Do you expect me to believe you did this out of love? Your husband carried vital information within his mind. Classified information of the utmost importance. Things he, in hindsight, should not have been privy to. He was rather adamant about reporting such things, which is why you find yourself the widow you are today. Rick carried a sickness. It's the sickness of thinking you have to do what you think is right no matter what. The problem is, his perception of what was right differed from ours." The old man laughed. His voice was dry and raspy. "The bit about being a hero is always for the public. Optics are everything. Dead and done is how we dealt with him." He cleared his throat. "But not quite dead or done, are we? You brought him back to us. And it's just a matter of time before those latent memories of his surface, and that is what we're after. We need those memories, Mrs. Crowberg." He leaned forward. Smiled. "Help us bring him in, Ellen. May I call you Ellen? I can make sure you live out the rest of your days rather than die the horrible death we have in store for you."

"I don't believe you." Her voice remained calm. Rick would have been proud of her.

The ancient agent of unknown rank ran his fingers across his bald head as if hair still occupied it. He smiled again; it was a smile that would send chills down anyone's back. "You've committed heinous crimes against our great and God-fearing nation. If you have any shred of patriotism left in you, you will help us."

"No. I brought him back because I love him. I needed him. My Rick. I have nothing to do with whatever you're talking about." She fought back the tears as best she could.

"Bring him to us." His smile turned menacing. "Just help bring him to us, and everything will be okay."

"I can't help you. Even if I could, my answer would still be no." Her strength was undeniable. She would not betray the man she loved.

"I did not want it to come to this Ellen. But you leave me no choice." The old agent's smile grew deeper, revealing yellow teeth of various shades.

The door to the interrogation room opened again, illuminating the dim surroundings to a greater degree. Another man entered wearing the same type of suit as the other agent. The striking difference with the second agent was that he carried a needle in his left hand.

"What is that?!" Ellen cried out.

"Last chance." The old agent's yellow teeth glistened in the added light from the open door.

"I don't know what you're talking about." Ellen did her best to back away from the needle, but the restraints kept her glued to the interrogation chair.

"I will find out the truth!" Spittle flew from the old man's mouth as he slammed his fist on the stainless-steel tabletop.

The focused pinprick of the syringe needle on her neck hurt; the agent didn't handle the injection with care like Doctor Potock had countless times. It released the chemical into her system, and it didn't take long for her to become less lucid. Self-control vanished from her will. She was at the mercy of those holding her captive.

* * * *

Deep within the lush and expansive forests of middle America, where state lines had been redrawn after the Second Civil War, a hidden camp of rebel clones lived, loved, and trained for a common purpose: freedom. This clandestine enclave, born out of resistance against the powerful and authoritarian regime named the Division of Illegal Cloning, was a marvel of covert engineering and strategic camouflage.

Camp Rebirth nestled within a natural amphitheater surrounded by towering ancient trees, their leaves forming a dense canopy that shielded the rebel clones from advanced satellite surveillance. In a race to repair the environment, towering redwoods and ancient oaks were erected to replace the lost forest lands. This type of cloning didn't raise any alarms. The newly established trees served as a natural barrier, concealing the camp and dampening any electronic signals that might give away its location. A wide net of camouflage shielding acted as a second defense against the peering eyes of the Division from above.

Over time, the outlawed clones mastered the art of blending technology with nature. They constructed the structures in the camp from advanced adaptive materials that mimicked the colors and textures of the surrounding environment. The buildings seamlessly integrated into the forest, appearing as nothing more than natural formations to the untrained eye.

To further avoid detection, the rebels utilized advanced anti-surveillance technology. Invisible dampening fields distorted the view of any intruding aerial drones, making the camp appear as an illusion amid the trees; this acted as the third defense. The rebel clones also developed a sophisticated system of signal jamming and electronic countermeasures to disrupt any attempts at high-tech reconnoitering.

Inside the camp, the clones trained rigorously, honing their combat skills and perfecting guerrilla tactics. The rebels nourished themselves with sustainable agriculture and aquaponics. This minimized their impact on the surrounding ecosystem. Renewable energy sources powered the camp, leaving no detectable energy signature that could betray their location.

They conducted communication through encrypted channels, and scouts equipped with state-of-the-art stealth technology patrolled the perimeter, ensuring the camp remained hidden. The combination of advanced technology and a deep understanding of the natural world allowed the resistance to thrive in secrecy, evading detection and remaining a beacon of hope for those deemed less than human.

Rick's clone crouched behind a small hill; his position gave him a view of the camp. Rick smiled as a few clones talked and laughed within the elegant hideout. He understood they were clones and noted that each had a shaved head. There was more to it than that. He somehow connected with his own kind. Felt them. As his mind wandered, he garnered feelings of what it meant to be home. It felt like home until he felt something else entirely: a gun barrel to the back of his head.

"I would have thought, given your record, a guy like me would never have been able to sneak up on a guy like you." Bartly chuckled while holding Rick at gunpoint. "Stand up."

"Well, I guess things aren't always as they appear." Rick stood up with the weapon fixed to the back of his head. Once again, the body remembered while the mind did not, and Rick's mind stood in awe as his body disarmed his aggressor with ease.

"Son of a bitch!" Bartly lay on his back, embarrassed at having his own firearm aimed at his head. "You are as good as everyone says. My name is Bartly. My given name was Matthew Drafton. That was the name of the man they created me after. I gave it up and took on my own name. I remember much of Matthew's life, but those are his memories. Mine are my own. You come from the one named Rick. Do you keep his name, or have you chosen one for yourself yet?"

More footsteps caused Rick to take a few cautious steps back. He kept both this Bartly and the man approaching him in his sight. The gun stayed synchronized with his eyes. He didn't experience nervousness. There was a calmness in Rick's bones he didn't understand. He knew he could fire with ease if he had to.

"Is this a normal way to welcome an invited guest?" Rick asked.

"Please forgive Bartly. Even though I advised him against it, he wanted to test you. My chosen name is Agson. Please put the weapon down. I extend a hand of friendship and trust rather than pointing a gun at you." Agson glared at Bartly for a split second as he reached his hand to Rick.

Rick pulled the magazine from the firearm and dismantled

the weapon as though he had done it a million times; he most likely had. Rick reached out for Agson's hand and shook it.

Bartly stood. "He's damn good. Could show me a thing or two."

"I was kind of hoping it would be the other way around. I'm tired of running to nowhere." Rick relaxed his guard. Deep down inside, he recognized these people were no threat to him.

"That is why we're here. Welcome." Agson smiled the smile he always smiled when bringing a new edition into the ranks.

* * * *

"She's not talking." The older, more experienced bald agent eyed his two colleagues, Li and Jones. Their identical black suits added to the ominous demeanor of the three. Jones and Li stood before the experienced agent as though he were a wise prophet, guiding them to the Promised Land. The man was ancient, and it was rumored he had been there at the inception of the Division of Illegal Cloning. He had rounded up the first clone and executed him himself.

"Perhaps she told the truth?" Li admitted. He sauntered to the one-way mirror and studied the beaten and crushed human who had once been a proud and beautiful Ellen Crowberg. She could barely sit on the rough metal bed in her cell. "God knows she'll never be the same after what we've done to her. She shouldn't have cloned the bastard in the first place. She should have left him for dead."

"Is that sympathy I detect in your voice?" Jones grew amused. His partner never spoke in such a way. The dark sunglasses on Jones' face hid the surprise in his eyes.

"More like pity." Li sighed and returned to face his fellow agents as they stood in one of several corridors in the Division of Illegal Cloning headquarters. "We've lost too much time already. We need to move fast. We must find Rick."

"More than likely, this Clone Liberation picked him up by now. There's no way in hell one of their own is in the wilderness for this long without them knowing about it." Jones' face flushed red with anger and frustration. "We had the bastard! He still evaded capture in his own home, of all places!"

"It does us no good to dwindle on past mistakes." The older agent of unknown rank studied the two novices in comparison. "Do whatever you must but find him. Fast. And remember not to underestimate him. He's just as elite now as when he was alive as the original Rick."

"We don't even know where to start," Li admitted begrudgingly. "We've been searching around the clock. He's vanished in the Reconstituted Forest."

"We have to assume his memories are resurfacing by now or will soon. He'll find out why he died." Jones crossed his arms, pondering. "That won't be good for anyone."

The older agent smiled; his yellow teeth glimmered in the light. "On the contrary, it's good for us. That is exactly what I am counting on, gentlemen." He ran his fingers across his bald head. "We'll use her to get to him. We'll use every last one of those memories that makes him remember why he loves her so damn much. He cares, and we can use that against him."

* * * *

Patrick expressed a genuine smile from ear to ear. The removal of hair was a vital ceremony that meant all ties from his previous life were severed, and the skin on his shaved head experienced the rush of a cool forest breeze. Certain things continued to be new experiences for his body, but old ones for his mind. Rick was the man he came from, and slight memories cropped up of who and what Rick was, but the clone chose the name Patrick. This was now his chosen name.

Bartly grinned and began the applause. The rest of the

clones joined in; the clapping of hands grew in enthusiastic intensity. Agson was the first to shake Patrick's hand, and Patrick went down the line, saying his thanks to everyone attending the ceremony. Men and women who adapted their lives to their new identities all gave him warm, comforting smiles, and those smiles reassured Patrick. This was home. These were his people.

"It feels good to finally be yourself, doesn't it, Patrick?" Agson asked while meeting Patrick's firm handshake for a second time. It was no mystery Agson took a particular interest in the one that was Rick, and as they spoke to each other, Agson led Patrick farther into the forest and away from the celebration.

"It sure does, sir," Patrick said.

"Enough with the sir business already. That's the way Rick would have addressed me. On the other hand, Patrick is a friend and familiar to me as friends are," Agson corrected.

Patrick smiled. "You got it Agson."

They would remember this day as Patrick's true birthday. People drank, some danced, and the joys of pregnancy overtook others. One of the female clones brought to the camp showed signs of the soon-to-be infant by the size of her belly. A community of people who weren't supposed to be alive was being born in the wilderness.

"Patrick. There's something I would like to speak to you about." Agson gestured for the man to follow him to a more secluded location near the camouflaged perimeter of the camp.

"I may not have known you for long, Agson, but I recognize the look on your face. You're about to ask me to do something rather unpleasant." Patrick sighed, bracing for the inevitable.

"You've been a part of the community for several months now. And we are blessed not only with your presence but also with the skills and knowledge you've offered to us all." Agson admitted.

Patrick nodded, waiting for the other shoe to drop. "I'm grateful for being able to help our kind."

Agson sighed before continuing. "The DIC discovered you so fast because of who you came from. They're afraid of you because of the latent memories that have yet to surface. And I would be lying to you if I told you those memories were anything but valuable to me as well."

Patrick shrugged, helpless. "I can't remember much. I can show some of these people how to be soldiers, but I'm afraid that's about it. I remember nothing else, Agson."

Agson locked eyes with Patrick. "You know more than you think. Buried in that mind of yours is proof. It's proof of something only Bartley, me, and a few others are privy to. Patrick, our nation's President, is a clone like you and I."

Patrick took a shocked step backward. "What? How can that be? I don't remember anything like that."

Agson reached into his pocket to reveal a small silver device. It appeared to be a visor in design meant to fit with ease over an individual's eyes. "This will retrieve what we need and save it. It can help you remember. I must warn you, though, that the process is less than pleasant. And I am asking you to do this for us. I'm not forcing you. The choice is yours."

Patrick studied the device. Rick experienced extreme torture throughout his career. Rick's ultimate experience was death itself. This was the least Patrick could do for the memory of Rick and the others like him. If Rick died knowing such an earth-shattering truth, it was Patrick's duty to retrieve the information. If what Agson described was true, the world needed to know it. "I'll do it."

With the hands of a surgeon, Agson placed the device over Rick's eyes. After pressing a button, the silver visor turned on, and Agson monitored the progression of the device's function as Patrick's body jolted about while he stood upright. Agson felt empathy for Patrick. The memory retrieval was as painful to watch as it had been to undergo all those years ago.

The deed was done minutes later, and Agson hastily removed the device from Patrick's face. Patrick's eyes were wide with knowledge as he focused on Agson. "I remember it Agson! I remember it all! My God, I remember! They knew I wouldn't keep quiet about it. Rick - he planned to let the world know."

Patrick did his best to maintain his strength and balance on wobbly legs.

Agson grimaced. "I'm sorry you had to experience that. Reliving the death is the hardest part."

Patrick shook his head. "Don't be. We needed the information, and now you have it all stored away in that visor."

* * * *

Bartly entered Agson's tent in a controlled flurry of motion. He stood at attention, unable to shake the habit that his body remembered from the time before Bartly when he was the one that came from Matthew. "Agson. The messenger is back." Bartly also gave Patrick a nod as he stood near Agson, going over final plans. He smirked as Patrick nodded in response.

"Let's not waste any time." Agson took a step forward. "Bring him in."

A skinny boy no older than seventeen entered the tent. He wore the same military fatigues all the clones wore. They were designed to blend into a forest environment, prioritizing advanced technology, adaptive materials, and stealth capabilities. The high-tech uniforms were crafted to provide optimal camouflage, protection, and mobility for soldiers of Camp Rebirth operating in their familiar dense woodland settings. The boy saluted Agson, tired from his journey and ready to relay the new information he had gathered.

"What did you find out?" Agson stood near the boy.

The boy cleared his throat and stood taller before speaking. "They're cracking down on all clone sympathizers. They have arrested anyone suspected of aiding clones for trial and execution. And these executions are going to be made public. They will carry them out tomorrow at the old football stadium."

"What?!" Patrick grew outraged. "Why would they do that? They're taking this too far!"

"They're desperate, Patrick. They want to get their hands on you. This is no doubt a trap put in place to bait you." Agson paced back and forth as he pondered the new information and returned his gaze to the boy. "Do you have anything else to report?"

The skinny boy nodded. "Our contact penetrated the central security systems of the targeted facilities. We can move in and out across the board now. Our contact informed me there wasn't anything left to stop us from realizing the plan. Everyone is waiting for you to give the final word. Our numbers are greater than what we have fed to the DIC."

"It's about time!" Bartly couldn't hide the joy he felt. He was ready to act. "They'll have to listen to us now."

"You did well, son." Agson placed his hands on the shoulders of the skinny boy in an approving manner. "You did very well. Now, get some rest. We're about to begin."

The skinny boy nodded and exited the tent.

"Bartly." Agson turned to face his longtime companion. "Spread the word. It's time to mobilize. The moment we've all been training for is here. We're going in as soon as we're ready. The first signal should be relayed within the next twenty hours."

"You got it." Bartly exited the tent to do as ordered.

"I can't go." Patrick averted his gaze, ashamed to make eye contact with Agson.

Agson nodded, understanding. "I had a feeling that it might come to this. You must know that they are counting on this reaction you're having right now. It's a trap to get you. They know you'll know that Ellen will be with the group scheduled for execution."

Patrick fought with his previous identity. Both versions agreed on one thing: they cared deeply for Ellen. "She's still alive. I remember loving her, and I'd be lying if I said I didn't still love her. I have to save her if I can." Patrick's voice never sounded so confident. "And that isn't just Rick's memories speaking. It's me, Patrick, voicing those feelings."

"Many people will die in what's coming. You could be of

great use to us still." Agson pleaded.

The idea of leaving tore at Patrick, but his decision was resolute. "You have Bartly. He's more than competent, and you now have a lot of excellent people trained and ready to go. Not to mention that you're leading them and are one hell of a leader."

A pang of sorrow filled Agson's chest as he gazed at Patrick. He understood this would more than likely be their last conversation. "Good luck to you, Patrick. I hope you find her and escape."

Patrick smiled; it was forced. "We'll both be around to celebrate when this is all over."

Agson watched with weary eyes as Patrick exited the tent to meet his fate.

* * * *

Ellen's last meal was comprised of chicken, rice, corn, a slice of bread, and a bland cola not of her choosing. She ate it with slow, deliberate bites, savoring the taste of the food as though a gourmet chef had prepared it. Armed guards escorted her down a long corridor following the main course, ripping her from a warm, unfinished meal. They had shaved her head the previous day to shame her. By doing so, it categorized her with the clones that eluded capture.

Thoughts of Rick floated through her mind as the guards took her to a massive room where a table extended from the metal floor. Behind the table sat three judges dressed in elegant robes. Each one was no older than Doctor Potock and carried eyes of extreme judgment as they studied her.

They determined her guilt with ease. The verdict was no surprise. Not even the death sentence came as a surprise.

Like cattle, they herded her from the courtroom with other clone sympathizers and people who had violated the law, hoping to regain time with a lost love or family member.

My God! It's a mass execution! The reality of it shocked what remained of her humanity.

The compartments in the back of the truck filled as each prisoner filed in one after another. They then made the vast number of prisoners travel without a word spoken amongst them. Each carried a grim face, as they all knew that they were about to face death.

* * * *

Agent Jones and Li both stood in one of the former VIP suites inside the now archaic football stadium. Within the grand structure where mighty sports teams once took the field, prisoners now walked. They packed the grounds of unkept turf, waiting for the last moments before they would be no more, and they paced back and forth, pleading to the sky with desperate glances for a miracle to save them.

Li studied the booth, wondering what it must have been like when this place had been meant for joyful events. I'm sure they had their problems back then. He let the thought drift as he eyed his partner.

"What's the matter with you?" Jones asked without turning back at Li. "I can always feel it when you look at me like that."

Li shrugged. "I was just thinking about how things used to be, that's all."

Jones chuckled. "You should look at how they're doing. All these damn sympathizers will soon be dead. If that isn't a clear enough message, I don't know what is. It's too bad this stadium isn't filled with all those damn clones."

The signal had been broadcast and transmitted to the device implanted beneath the skin of his right wrist. Li's time had come. The message was loud and clear, and all deep undercover operatives had been activated. The clones would be liberated, and Agent Li would play his part unbeknownst to Agent Jones.

"Yeah," Li smiled, "those clones sure are a big pain in the ass."

Agent Jones chuckled again while turning to face his partner. The smile vanished as he stared at the barrel of a government-issued sidearm. "Li, what the hell are you doing?!"

Li smirked. "I chose a long time ago, same as you."

"We are partners!" Jones bellowed. "When the fuck did you become a goddamn clone sympathizer?!"

Li chuckled this time. "We were never really partners, Jones. I'm just a damn clone. The kind you love so much to hate. The original Li - he died a while ago."

It was a silent gunshot that ended the life of Agent Jones. It was also a silent signal transmitted from Li to all the other operatives in the area, informing them that the final liberation had begun. Operation Second Life took the country by storm.

* * * *

Ellen shuffled about amongst the prisoners with no direction, trying to anticipate how their collective lives would end. While mixing with other groups of people, she noted a familiar face in the sea of gray uniforms.

"Doctor Potock!" Her voice couldn't help but express the relief of knowing he still lived, and a dark sadness blanketed her entire being. They were both going to die soon.

Potock turned his head in her direction. The old man appeared strange with a shaved head. He embraced her as a father would a daughter. "Ellen! My God, I was so worried about you!"

She fought back tears. "I'm glad you're here! I thought I'd die alone."

"We share this fate together, my dear." The sentiment strangely reassured them both.

Strength returned to Ellen at that moment. "Yes, we do."

A light began flashing throughout the stadium. The dome overhead closed, stealing their last view of the sky above.

Then, a series of perfectly timed explosions occurred throughout the stadium, creating a mass hysteria. The prisoners were unclear whether the explosions were intentional. Soon enough, they began running about frantically, piling upon one another to find some semblance of safety as debris fell around them and the massive structure groaned from the vibrations.

Potock held on to Ellen and grew surprised to feel another firm hand grab onto his own. Shock couldn't begin to describe Potock's face as he beheld a bald Rick standing before him. "Rick..."

"Hello, Doctor. It's good to see you again. We have to go right now." Patrick stood before the two, wearing the same gray uniform as the rest of the prisoners. "Another set of charges is about to go off. It'll give us the diversion we need to escape. Come with me."

Giving into the moment, Ellen ran to her husband and embraced him with all her strength. She kissed him, unleashing a pent-up passion as the mass hysteria enveloped their environment, and soon found she was melting in his loving arms as if nothing else in the world was going on. "I knew you'd come back for me. I never gave up hope."

"Your hope kept me alive," Patrick admitted.

Ellen's smile deepened.

The clone led Potock and Ellen through a corridor into an old locker room in the stadium. The second set of explosions went off with a violent boom, and they fell to the ground as the surrounding structure shook from the mini-quake that followed.

"The other people, are they okay?" Ellen voiced the question on her mind. She had been scheduled to die with them, after all.

"I did my best to make sure the explosions wouldn't harm anyone. But given the hysteria out there, I can't say for certain no one was hurt or killed. But we can't worry about that right now. We have to keep moving." Patrick explained.

Ellen nodded, experiencing a tinge of immense guilt at being happy for still being alive as others around her died. She did her best to shake the emotion as she, Potock, and Rick rounded a corner in the locker room. Upon making the turn to the exit of the stadium, a fatal gunshot echoed.

Time slowed down as Ellen observed in a helpless state as Potock's body hit the ground.

"Ellen, my dear, did you honestly think this would end well for any of you?" The older agent stood before them. Like Ellen remembered, his bald head and skin were covered in liver spots. His black suit blended into the shadows near where he stood. His presence loomed over Rick and Ellen like the darkest of clouds.

"You..." A rage grew within her, the likes of which she had never experienced.

Before Ellen could even think about acting, another gunshot went off. Ellen hit the floor with a hand covering a bullet wound in her gut; the blood seeped from her stomach like tears running down her cheeks. A third gunshot followed. Patrick hit the floor of the abandoned locker room as well.

"Ellen..." Patrick crawled to her as she lay bleeding. He spoke with a weak voice. "I remember. I wanted you to know that I remember everything, and I wanted to tell you I love you so much. I needed to look you in the eye and say it one more time."

Before any words could be spoken in response, life faded from Ellen Crowberg's eyes. Soon after witnessing her death, Patrick ceased moving altogether. This was the second time Rick/Patrick died for what he believed in. The first was for an honor-bound code preventing conspiracy, and the second was for love.

The ancient agent towered over the bodies in a victorious stance. He spoke into his wrist while staying vigilant about any unexpected escapees. "We got him. Repeat: the primary target is down." A devilish grin formed on his face.

Another voice responded in his earpiece. "Copy that. Stand by. It looks like we've got situations brewing all over the country. Attacks are being made everywhere. Report to Division HQ immediately."

* * * *

President Brandon Tej sat behind his desk in the Oval Office, dressed in a finely tailored suit, awaiting a critical meeting. The clone rebellion had been well organized and took much manpower to contain, but President Tej understood the word contain was a misnomer. The events leading up to now had been more like a ceasefire, at best. This Operation Second Life, orchestrated by the clones, shook the nation's fabric.

The Oval Office had undergone a transformation, reflecting advancements in technology, design, and sustainability. Smart glass walls lined the perimeter, capable of transitioning from transparent to opaque with a simple voice command or touch interface. This feature provided President Tej with privacy when needed while maintaining a connection to the outside world.

They equipped the office with holographic displays that could project three-dimensional images. This enabled President Tej to interact with virtual data, briefings, and simulations, creating an immersive and dynamic workspace. They integrated the augmented reality surface on his desk with digital information. This interactive surface allowed the President to manipulate data, review reports, and engage in virtual meetings with a simple touch or gesture. His next meeting, however, would be face-to-face.

A voice broke the silence with a knock at the door. One of Tej's agents stepped in, looking at his commander and chief. "Mr. President. We've brought him in to see you."

Tej sighed. "Bring him in." He straightened out his shirt and suit jacket.

Agson smiled fondly, remembering what it was like to be in this office from his previous life. The restraints binding him as the agent led him in were a bit much for this meeting, but he understood they had to keep up appearances for the sake of politics. *Power perceived and all that.*

"Sit him down," Tej ordered, waiting until Agson sat across from him before continuing. "Now leave us."

The agent gave the President a questioning glance, and Tej met the gaze even harder, reminding the agent of his position. The agent nodded and exited the office with reluctance.

Agson nodded. "Hello, Mr. President. It's good to see you again."

Tej said nothing.

"I love what you've done with the place," Agson continued.

Tej grumbled before speaking. "You've been keeping quite busy."

Agson nodded in agreement. "I had to pass the time somehow."

President Tej cleared his throat before continuing. "You have the memories hidden somewhere. I want the original copy you took from Richard Crowberg."

Agson gave the President a disappointed glare. "I know what you want, Brandon."

Tej grumbled again. "It's President Tej."

Agson cleared his throat and landed forward. "No, actually it isn't. We both know that the real Tej died. Look, Brandon, we stopped this skirmish before it got too far. But you understand, we will go as far as it takes to make this right. We're the ones who stopped the attacks, and they can just as easily be started up again." Agson held up his hands, offering the restraints holding them. "These are for appearance. They don't really hold me back."

Tej exploded with anger. "For Christ's sake, Barry, we were friends!"

Agson shook his head. "Barry died. He was the Secretary of Defense during your first administration. I'm just plain old Agson these days."

Tej considered his options and relented. "What do you want?"

Agson continued. "I want the policy on clones to be lifted, and I want my people to have a real chance to live normal, happy lives. We'll start with a separate community first. Think of it as a way for these people to start fresh without outside interference. Integration will have to happen eventually, but we need to take baby steps before we get there."

Tej laughed. "And who are you to dictate policy to me?"

Agson sighed, tired of the back and forth. "I'm just another clone, like you. If these demands aren't met, there will be another attack and a different ending to this story than I would like. Those memories you desperately want will go public as well."

Tej stood from the chair behind his desk; the frantic energy building within him had no outlet. The road ahead would be difficult, but he understood what he had to do. Too much was at stake. His presidency was in jeopardy, and many more innocent lives could be lost if he failed to navigate appropriately.

"What is it going to be?" Agson asked, smiling the smile he always smiled when adding a new edition to the ranks.

MY LOVELY MACHINE ELF

STORY 10

"ARE YOU SURE this stuff is safe, Rick?" Daniel studied the drink. He questioned the judgment of his childhood friend as he often did at times like this. Rick called it a strange name Daniel never heard of, and as a result, ayahuasca was the word repeating in his obsessive mind. Where Rick acquired the narcotic made Daniel curious, but in reality, it didn't concern him. Rick's greatest strength was his talent for obtaining what could or should not be obtained.

"Just enjoy it." Tall, slender, and shaggy-haired served as an accurate depiction of Rick, who was only twenty years of age. He moseyed to Daniel with a childish gate and placed his plastic cup on the coffee table with delicate grace. After, he sank into the dilapidated foldout couch; this couch accompanied him through the first years of college. He motioned with a welcoming gesture for his best friend to sit beside him.

"I'm not sure about this." Daniel hesitated before sitting, putting his cup next to Rick's.

"I'm telling you, Danny, you're going to trip like never before, and you are going to love every God damned second of it!" The excitement animated Rick's entire body as he wiggled about. "Yes, I've been looking for the perfect high, and this cup, my special brew, ranks at the top of the list, my friend. Now I'm your stoner buddy. I understand this, as do you, but you must also let go occasionally. It'd do you some good to break from being the cooped-up little bookworm."

Daniel sighed, taking the comment to heart. He despised when Rick referred to him as a bookworm. Daniel also understood his delicate build and slender frame did little to attract the opposite sex. Consuming himself with his studies curved this line of thought. "I'm not a bookworm, Rick. I care about my future, unlike you."

"Now, that's not a nice thing to say. Of course, I care about my future. And in the future, I see the two of us taking a fantastic trip. No bullshit. This stuff will send us up to the fuckin' moon and back. I mixed it with all the right ingredients, just how the man told me to." Rick's eager smile awaited Daniel's response.

"Who the hell did you get this from?" Daniel's paranoia defined so much of his existence; it ate its way into the current situation.

Rick struggled to remember. "I met him at a party the other night." Rick shrugged, having spent as much energy as he was willing to on the matter. "I tried some of it then, and it was... It was beyond words, man." The recollection of the high shot a sense of euphoria throughout Rick's body.

Daniel grew concerned. "And you trust this guy? You don't even know his name, do you?"

"Names are overrated!" Rick countered. "And besides, where do you think I got the stuff in the first place? I didn't pull it out of my ass. This guy is intense. He couldn't wait to share the experience with others, so I figured I'd give it a go." Rick smiled again and took a deep, relaxing breath. "Now, are we gonna talk all damn night nitpicking, or are we going to do this?"

Defeated, Daniel shrugged in agreement. "One time won't hurt, I guess."

"Yes! This is the Daniel I know and love!" Rick wasted no time lifting his cup from the coffee table and chugging the special tea.

Daniel took a moment to study the eclectic apartment while gingerly lifting the red solo cup into his hands. The unmistakable scent of marijuana lingered in the air; even though Daniel did not smoke, he found the aroma calmed his more obsessive-compulsive tendencies. Rick also loved his incense candles, which helped create a more relaxing atmosphere or momentary nausea depending on what odors were mixed together.

Daniel's more tidy tendencies could easily be spotted; book-shelves were filled with diverse literature, from academic texts to the latest horror novels. The beanbag chair in the living room corner suited them both: Rick enjoyed passing out on it, and Daniel found it a comfortable option for losing himself in a book.

Strings of fairy lights hung overhead and along the walls. Rick insisted on this lighting scheme; it provided a mellow and invit-ing atmosphere. The tapestries along the walls were a mix of stoner culture nicknacks and posters that spoke to Rick. Daniel's influences were dotted throughout Rick's more aggressive interi-or design approach: posters from his favorite movies, collector's editions of sci-fi/fantasy books, and various collectible Funko Pop figures from films, anime, and games added a complimen-tary contrast. Eclectic furniture accumulated over the years; none matched very well but spoke to their immediate need for furni-ture and Rick and Daniel's refusal to invest in proper furnish-ings.

The most prized corner of the room was set up for gaming and music. A collection of diverse vinyl records rested in milk crates on bricks as a makeshift shelf. High-end speakers con-nected to an older record player immersing Rick in whichever album he played. The gaming system was state-of-the-art; Daniel built the gaming PC and tinkered with upgrades when necessary. Escaping into another reality was something Daniel excelled at, and the gaming universe satiated the need to be someone else for a while.

"What the hell are you waiting for? Drink up!" Rick slapped Daniel on the back, taking him from his moment of extreme observation. Rick smiled and gazed straight ahead at nothing in particular as he waited for the full effects of the drug-infused beverage to kick in.

Daniel placed the cup to his lips with a weary sigh and allowed the liquid to pour down his throat; it coated his insides with a familiarity he found unsettling. Before Daniel knew it, Rick tipped the end of the cup upward, causing him to chug all the tea.

Startled, Daniel threw the cup forward while gasping for air. "What the fuck?!" He held his throat while choking; it subsided after a few seconds.

"Don't worry, man! Go with it!" A smile from ear to ear adorned Rick's face.

Daniel stood in the apartment's living room, pacing around while doing his best to gather his senses. Strange couldn't describe the sensations emanating from his conscious and subconscious awareness. The euphoric warmth wrapped his body and soul with a sensitivity beyond any verisimilar reality he experienced before. It also left a sliver of consciousness open, reminding him with an intense fervor that this state of existence has always been lying dormant within the confines of his soul. This tantalizing yet eerie lack of perturbation awaited his arrival with a graceful love. It called to him with a song whose notes were the epitome of home.

Daniel focused on Rick, who was already in his own world and still seated on the couch. "Rick. I feel... It's..." Words failed Daniel as the potent concoction took control.

The room swirled. The colors blended and transformed in unimaginable combinations. Daniel experienced his entire body being transferred to another place where shapes collided, and the laws of the universe disregarded every theory posted by the world's foremost scientific minds. The surrounding walls oscillated as if they carried a pulse all their own, and with little effort, he tasted the varying colors around him.

This is crazy! The thought echoed audibly as he explored his new reality. *Yellow! I can taste the color yellow!*

A humanoid figure coalesced from the jumbled shapes before him, and Daniel smiled as he regarded the approaching creature. Her shape pulsed with the rhythm of the oscillating walls, and her flesh combined with the colors in fantastical arrangements. Her ears were pointed, and the hair upon her head was a brilliant blonde that ran the spectrum of shades. She gave Daniel a warm smile while appearing in many places around him at once.

Who are you? Your color tastes so lovely. Daniel's thought echoed in this realm as if he were speaking.

As do your colors, Daniel. I am your reality. Without me, you could not exist. Nothing in your world would exist. We dance. We dance the dance which holds the fabric of the universe together. Her voice soothed and comforted as it echoed within and around Daniel. Her taste was intoxicating; the arousal within his jeans intensified to where he thought he might orgasm.

I'd love to taste the color of your hair. There are so many colors here. They all taste so wonderful. This is all so wonderful. Daniel said.

Her laugh was welcoming as she continued to phase in and out of various spots in the surreal landscape surrounding Daniel.

What are you? He asked.

We are your world, Daniel. We have been waiting for you. Her voice was the song that created worlds.

Daniel swiveled his head in every direction and returned his gaze to the creature, confused. *What do you mean? You're the only one I see here.*

You must dance. To stay here, you must dance the dance and keep things together. We create balance. You are one of us. You always have been. As she spoke, the scent of her smile created a hunger in Daniel's soul.

Quite suddenly, Daniel felt the creature merge with his being, and he was enveloped by the light surrounding her. His soul entangled in an odd mixture of pleasure going far beyond the erotic and into the realm of ecstasy in its highest form. In the simplest terms available, it had been a dance of light and darkness. It was a dance of balance where everything was connected, and nothingness brought forth all the possibilities of the universe.

Focus on nothing, and you focus on everything! The thought flowed and echoed repeatedly as Daniel danced with the lovely creature. He hadn't a clue if it was his own thought or the creature's, but he could move everywhere by submitting. It was a trip he wished would never, ever end. As the dancing grew more intense, he felt an explosion in his loins; the release cleared his mind, and as he shivered, he could feel the strange female creature caressing his soul.

* * * *

It had been one week since the life changing experience. Daniel did his best to return to the everyday routines and rigors of college life but lacked the determined enthusiasm that was once readily available. Rick informed his best friend the encounter was nothing to be alarmed about. The term used to describe the otherworldly creature was machine elf. The conversation played repeatedly in Daniel's mind as he sat in his history class, zoning off into the memory of the intangible experience.

"Machine elf? What the hell is that?" Daniel grew confused and crashed hard from the high. He lay sprawled about on the apartment floor, hypnotized by the fairy lights above and yearning to return to the place of pure bliss.

"That's what some dead old dude called them, or some shit like that. I think his name was Terence McKenna, if I'm not mistaken. Anyway, they're supposed to be these fucking elves that exist in this altered state of reality. Freaky shit. Kind of makes the old wheel turn." Rick chuckled while lying on the foldout couch and pointed a finger to his head in a circular motion.

"You almost sounded like some kind of intellectual for a second." Daniel laughed, still sensing the remnants of the sweet nirvana.

"No shit, hey?" Rick took it as a compliment.

Daniel began laughing with an unhealthy cadence. "I need to go back there, Rick. I have to go back!"

"Go back? What the hell are you talking about?" Rick sat up on the couch, sinking in, and eyed his companion. "You never left the apartment, you fuckin' twat."

"No." Daniel kept his eyes fixed on the ceiling. "You don't understand. I left. I was somewhere else for a little while."

"I don't follow." Rick reached for a cigarette. The pack had been on the coffee table next to him, where week-old Chinese food remained untouched. He packed it before picking one out at random.

"What existed before language? Words confine what is and what has been. We've done that as a species. We are more than the definitions we've created for ourselves. We're the manifestation of the universe." Daniel smiled, remembering the intensity of the orgasmic revelation.

After a few quick puffs from his American Spirit cigarette, Rick gave his friend a questioning glance. "What the hell are you going on about? Are you still high?"

Daniel sat up from his sprawled-out position, and his eyes were ablaze with the intensity of his words. "Rick, I have to go back. You can do that for me, can't you?"

Concern formed on Rick's face. "Ah shit, what have I created?"

Daniel rolled his eyes. "I'm being serious."

Rick shrugged, letting out a few more puffs. "Okay. Yeah, sure, I can do it. Relax. Let's say... same time next week?" Rick took another drag from his cigarette. "Sound good?"

"Yes!" Daniel smiled. "The universe is evolving, Rick. We're a part of that evolution."

"You're fuckin' crazy." Rick began laughing as he finished his cigarette.

The conversation faded from Daniel's mind as he raced home from class. He barreled through crowds of students and pedestrians and ran the final few blocks to his apartment from campus. Nothing could stop him. Nothing would stop him. He would reunite with his lovely machine elf.

After fumbling with his keys, Daniel burst into the apartment. A startled Rick nearly dropped his coffee mug and held his chest in relief. He placed the mug on the kitchen counter. "What the fuck, man?! I thought you were coming to collect or some shit!"

"Collect?" This confused Daniel.

"I may or may not owe someone money. No biggie. It's being handled." Rick assured his childhood friend. He stepped closer to Daniel. "So, do you think you'll handle this one without the freaky commentary after?"

It had gone unnoticed initially, but Daniel realized his friend was wearing black dress slacks and a nice blue shirt with an elaborate tie to match. It was an actual tie, not the clip-on ties Rick usually wore. His long hair was groomed, and the scent of aftershave directed you to a freshly shaved face, exposing a generous jawline. Rick cleaned himself up and made himself appear respectable. "Are you going somewhere?"

"I have employment now. I'm working as a waiter downtown. You didn't think I'd buy a tie like this, did you?" Rick cast an incredulous gaze.

"But I thought... I thought you were going to be here for this. I thought we'd do it together like the first time." Daniel failed to hide the disappointment in his voice.

"Believe me, Danny, there is nothing I'd love more than to watch you freak the fuck out again, but you're the one always going on and on about responsibility and shit. So here I go, becoming a productive member of society, and what do you want to do? You want to get me out of work so I can get high. I know my career choices are short-lived, but let's just see how long I can put up with a proper job. I'm going to give myself a month for this gig. Care to wager on it?" Rick smirked as he finished getting ready.

Daniel lifted his hand up in protest. "But-"

"Hey," Rick interrupted. "The tea is ready to go. It's in the kitchen. Pour yourself a glass or two and enjoy. Don't start going through my shit all high and whatnot. Time for me to get going. Don't want to be late again. It's my second day, after all."

Before Daniel could utter another word, his friend was out the door and locking it behind him. The need to fulfill the dance that now defined so much of him called to his soul. The tea was fresh, and he held the cup while standing in the kitchen. He took in the flavored scent of the concoction, allowing it to penetrate his nostrils, and after a quick sip, he downed the entire cup. A smile formed. He would soon be off into another realm, but before the full effects could take hold, he poured a second cup of tea and drank it as quickly as the first. This would be a trip Daniel would never forget.

The shapes and colors surrounded his senses like a swarm of locusts. Things phased in and out of reality, and he experienced that strange connection with everything that had been such an essential facet of his first trip in the altered reality. The air tasted sweet as he inhaled, and the colors were as vibrant as ever as the molecules before his eyes danced and connected to the rhythm of creation.

I can see it! I can see the atom! The idea of it excited Daniel.

Yes, and it is yours to dance with. The female creature of Daniel's first encounter glided near him, phasing in and out and appearing in many places at once.

How? Daniel turned to the elf creature, smiling. *You are so beautiful.*

Dance with me, Daniel. Dance with me. She reached for him.

Daniel felt the hands along his back even though she touched his chest. He gave himself to the female creature, surrendering everything that he was. She entered his essence, and his soul intertwined with the fabric of the elf. He was the atoms and the molecules. He was connected with everything through the empty spaces in the universe. His dance allowed reality to be. Without him, things would not exist. He found purpose. He found meaning. He found peace.

We are. Daniel's voice now sounded strange as he fell deeper and deeper into the realm of the elves. *We are. I am, but I do not exist. "I" is an illusion.*

Dance Daniel, the machine elf guided him. *Dance with us forever. You are with us forever. We build until others can come. Only then will the dance be no more. Until that time, we must keep dancing.* She insisted; the rhythm of creation grew to higher intensities.

Why me? Why did you choose me? He asked.

Daniel felt like he smiled as she smiled, even though his lips did not move. *You were receptive to us, Daniel. We knew you would be easy to bring in.*

Before his consciousness connected with the rest of the creature, he regarded globular shapes hovering in the distance. He wanted to reach out to these strange shapes but somehow understood they became out of reach. He became a part of this realm. His dancing kept the fabric of the universe together.

What is that? What are those shapes? Daniel asked.

The female elf soothed Daniel's unease. *Those are the ones we await. They have yet to cross over into our realm. One day, they will come here to dance as you have.*

Before the concept of language faded from Daniel's consciousness, he did his best to focus on one shape. For the briefest second, he could have sworn he viewed his body.

I don't like this anymore! Let me go! Daniel raged. The desperation did nothing to prevent the orgasmic euphoria, creating a confusing mix of pleasure and fear.

No Daniel. You cannot fight it. It is too late. You are meant to dance now until there is no more song. She explained.

With wild desperation, Daniel attempted to reconnect with his physical body; the elves of the surreal realm forced him back. The pain he now felt was ten times the ecstasy in reverse. Daniel would scream if he only had a voice. In the back of the consciousness that remained, he heard the female elf laughing with sadistic joy. The evil tone of laughter was so intense that if Daniel still had his body, he would have been petrified with fear.

Why? His thought was a whimper.

This is what we do, Daniel. This is how we become free of the dance. We've been dancing since the beginning. She explained. An edge of laughter remained in her tone.

If Daniel could have screamed, his shrieks would have been heard worldwide.

* * * *

"Will he ever wake up again?" Diane asked as she gazed upon her son with the loving eyes of a mother in pain. Daniel lay in the hospital bed of a room in the inpatient wing.

"There's no way to say with certainty. I'm sorry. If you wish, we'll move him to another section of the hospital where other patients with similar comas are being treated. Again, I'm sorry there isn't much more we can do. There's been an epidemic of young people falling into a coma from drug overdose lately. A lot have, thankfully, woken up. But I wouldn't want to give you false hope. All we can do is wait and see." Doctor Beckett turned from Daniel's parents. He exited the room, leaving the family to grieve in their own way.

"I don't understand. He was a good kid." Bruce looked at his son, gently running his fingers through his hair. A sense of gratefulness filled his soul at not having to have him hooked up to a respirator. Daniel was simply in a nonresponsive state.

"We need to give it time, Bruce. I'm sure he'll come out of it. He's a fighter." Diane spoke the words, trying to convince herself of the idea just as much as her husband. And while she monitored Daniel, she thought of all the hopes and dreams she secretly held for him. A tear fell from her eye and onto Daniel's hospital gown.

"You're right. Danny will come out of this. He'll bounce back and finish school. And he'll graduate, most likely with honors, knowing how much he studies." Bruce held back his own tears.

"He's got a bright future ahead of him." Diane held her husband's hand as they both took a seat near the hospital bed. They hoped beyond hope he could hear them and wanted nothing more than for him to awaken.

Their prayers had been answered.

Daniel's body began twitching as life returned to it. His eyes opened, and he regarded the world of flesh where substance was bound by physical laws. He soaked in the entire room with a childlike gaze as if seeing the world for the first time. Daniel's parents shot to their feet with tears of joy.

"Daniel?" Bruce asked. Hope elevated his tone.

"Where am I? Daniel's voice was weak. He sounded as if he were not used to speaking.

Bruce moved to hold his son's hand while looking behind him at the open door of the hospital room. "Doctor Beckett! Doctor Beckett, you need to get in here!" He turned back to his son. "Daniel, my God, you're okay! Thank God you're with us!"

"Daniel?" Daniel appeared confused. The name Daniel didn't register.

"Yes. You're our son, Daniel." Diane stood on the other side of her boy, holding his other hand just as tightly as his father.

"Yes. Daniel." The elf inhabiting the body smiled from ear to ear while regarding the parents of the vessel he took over. It was a common occurrence with the elves, and she waited a long time to be a part of this realm. All she had to do was act as though she carried no recollection of this vessel's life, and they would embrace him, filling in the missing information she needed to survive. They would all embrace her with open arms. *I am*

Daniel, the machine elf thought.

"You okay, son?" Bruce asked.

"Yes. I'm okay." Another smile formed on Daniel's face. "My name is Daniel."

BEYOND THE NORTH WIND

STORY 11

IT REACTIVATED. THE sensory input overwhelmed it at first. Processing the multitude of unknown sounds needing categorization became the first objective. It completed this task in half a second. Lighting levels changed in random patterns, making vision difficult, but it overcame the obstacle with indifferent efficiency and obtained vision again. Adjusting to lighting conditions proved to be another simple task, and the once foreign noises that created confusion formed a pattern. It remembered the idea of language within the massive memory stores of its consciousness. From what it ascertained, it had been confined within a wooden container. Now that it was becoming fully aware, the container became laughable. The wooden crate was useless as a means of confinement.

"What the fuck are we doing?" Ricky cast frightened glances at the crate.

"What we always do," Joey responded without missing a

beat. He stayed focused. They had a job, and he would ensure they did it.

Ricky and his childhood friend, Joey, smuggled many items men and women of note wanted to be hidden from prying eyes. However, Ricky never dreamed of transporting the type of cargo resting in the massive crate. He understood the monstrosity wasn't human, but he and Joey picked the strange thing up from a cargo ship at the docks, as they'd done a million times before with various other items.

The moon hung like a lantern in the night sky, casting an ethereal glow over the city's sprawling docks. The cargo ship, an imposing silhouette against the shimmering water, teased of secrets within its metal confines. Ricky and Joey waited at the berth for two men hidden by the shadows of the cargo ship.

When Ricky and Joey assisted with loading the thing into the custom wooden crate, he was confident it weighed the same as a full-grown man. The damn thing comprised arms, legs, hands, fingers, feet, and toes. The silver skin freaked Ricky out the most. The shimmering epidermis covering every inch of it carried the same texture as human skin, and where a face should have been, there was only more smooth silver skin. As they hauled the sealed wooden crate, now containing the item, to the nondescript black van, the air filled with the distant hum of industrial machinery and the occasional creaking of ship anchors.

"I don't like it." Ricky's voice almost trembled. He tried not to stare at the crate in the back of the van, but the contents mesmerized him. It purchased - no - stole and kept real estate in his mind.

"We're doing our job, Ricky. Just relax, will ya? We deliver like we've always done. Remember, we're getting paid a hell of a lot of money to make sure this thing gets to where it needs to get to." Joey spoke with a confidence he didn't quite feel. The silver-skinned freak unsettled him to the bone, as much, if not more, than it did with Ricky.

"When you told me about the money, Joey, I was all over it, but this thing in there.... It's not right. It ain't human, whatever the hell it is. I think it's alive. I don't like this one bit. It didn't have eyes, but I swear I could feel the fuckin' thing staring at me." Panic grew within Ricky.

Joey chuckled to his friend as he drove the worn and nondescript cargo van from the pickup point at the docks. The night hung heavy over the city as the van's engine broke the silence of the midnight streets; the headlights cut through the obscurity of dimly lit corners as the van navigated the labyrinth of factories and warehouses that loomed like sentinels upon entering the industrial district. The night swallowed the van as it weaved through the maze of deserted streets, avoiding the occasional flickering streetlights that threatened to expose its clandestine journey. Joey pushed the vehicle forward, finding comfort with the low hum created by the tires rolling on worn pavement. The van, now a specter in the night, blended seamlessly with its surroundings, leaving behind only the fading echoes of its passage through the industrial shadows.

"I'm telling you. Something ain't right." Ricky broke the moment of silence. The crate's contents alerted the most basic parts of his brain. Fright or flight kicked into overdrive.

"It's not alive Ricky! It's a fucking thing! That's what the guy who is paying us said." Joey forced anger to subdue his own doubts.

The crate rattled.

"Did you fuckin' hear that shit?" Ricky tried to create more space between him and the crate.

"Things make noises. Especially when they don't work right, and the thing back there doesn't work right. That's what our new employer said. Stick to the plan. Stop acting like a scared little bitch about it all." Joey said, putting up the front of a seasoned enforcer.

The noise grew more intense for a few seconds; the thing clawed at the wood holding it prisoner. Ricky kept his eyes on the crate, and his nervousness mingled with intense fear; his heart pounded with such force that Ricky heard it above the hum of the engine. The sweat poured from his forehead, and he reached for the gun in his waistband. The scratching intensified and backed off as if the thing was curious about the wood containing it.

"What are you doing?" Joey asked.

"Something ain't right." Ricky held his sidearm steady, keeping the Glock pointed at the crate. "If this fuckin' thing pops out, I'm going to pop it! Fuck the money!"

"Jesus Christ!" Joey kept his eyes on the dark streets they drove through.

When Joey turned left, the crate burst open, and Ricky went mad with gunfire.

* * * *

Alejandro understood life in the slums; he grew up in one. The neighborhood was a maze of poorly constructed housing projects and back-alley buildings that created tight streets and plenty of shady areas to conduct the type of business that generated ill-gotten gains. Alejandro was the oddity. He was a man in his mid-twenties with average intelligence. This didn't lead Alejandro to amount to much in life, but Alejandro kept his nose clean. He did honest work and tried his best to avoid the bad influences that consumed so many in the neighborhood he called home.

He approached bar close time at El Rincón. This was the corner bar where he served homegrown American drinks and Puerto Rican specialties to the mix of mainland-born and fresh off-the-island Puerto Rican clientele. These were the people that made up the neighborhood. He'd run into the occasional "tourist" from the suburbs or college kids looking to party away from anywhere their parents might frequent. Sometimes, the young outsiders wanted to experience the "real city." It never went the way they expected. On this night, he stopped one fight, flirted with a married woman, and caved into having a cigarette even though he swore to himself he would quit. Stress got to him; life, for Alejandro, grew more and more difficult as of late.

The air in El Rincón was thick with the lingering aroma of cheap cigars and the faint scent of spilled beer. No one here cared if you still smoked in the bar, but Alejandro policed it as best he could. No one in a position of authority came down to enforce it, anyway. The flickering neon lights outside cast a sporadic glow through the windows, highlighting the worn wooden tables and faded barstools. The tired floor creaked beneath his worn-out sneakers as he navigated between the tables, collecting empty glasses and wiping down surfaces. The chatter of the night's patrons dwindled, leaving only a few stragglers nursing their drinks in quiet corners.

A mix of camaraderie and weariness, reflective of the struggles the surrounding neighborhood residents faced, dampened the mood. Outside, the distant sounds of the city at night reverberated, punctuated by police sirens and the murmurs of conversations echoing through narrow alleyways. As Alejandro counted the day's earnings, the clinking of coins and the crumpling of bills and credit/debit card receipts filled the air. His face bore the weight of both responsibility and resilience, mirroring the struggles of the community he served. The bar, a sanctuary for locals seeking solace from the hardships of life, now needed to close its doors.

The neon sign above the entrance hummed its final glow as Alejandro locked the door, the click resonating through the empty streets. He glanced around one last time, ensuring everything was in order before slipping the keys into his pocket. The night was silent. The police liked to patrol around this time, and the shady deals that went down never happened in public. Only the idiots did things like that, and as Alejandro turned a corner into a narrow street, he cursed his luck. The shortcut he thought would take him home sooner delivered him to two such idiots.

A young blond man with ghostly pale skin, unexpected at this time of night in his community, smirked as if God had delivered him a fresh payday. Alejandro's tan skin, black hair, and frown contrasted with the physical appearance of the youth. A smile formed on the second young man's face; his dark black skin glowed under the alleyway light in the same ghostly fashion as the young white boy's. Their tattered clothing reeked, and some of their teeth were missing when they smiled. These two young men knew life on the streets, likely moving from neighborhood to neighborhood.

"You took a wrong turn, man." The blond kid spit on the ground before Alejandro.

"I don't want any trouble. I just want to go home." Alejandro took a step back.

"Don't move!" The blond kid pulled out a knife.

"Money! Now!" The black kid stepped up, tearing through Alejandro's pockets.

"I don't have much, but you're welcome to it," Alejandro said.

"No shit." The blond kid countered.

In the background, the sound of an out-of-control vehicle broke the typical silence these city dwellers grew accustomed to at two in the morning. All three turned in the direction from where Alejandro entered and were shocked as a massive black van slammed into a few parked cars as it sped without direction along the street. The van jumped the sidewalk to the already narrow street and scratched with furious rage against the side of the brick buildings, sending sparks of light into the night.

At that moment, Alejandro couldn't think. He couldn't even move. He closed his eyes and lost track of the young kids who sought an easy payday. He said a prayer as the bright light of the out-of-control black van came closer.

* * * *

The flickering light of the alleyway forced Alejandro to open his eyes. The moments before the impact of the van crashing were a blur and hazy at best. He studied his surroundings, attempting to orient himself. The black van had smashed like an accordion against the brick building across from him. The white kid didn't make it through the ordeal alive. His leg dangled from where the van and brick wall met, and Alejandro tried not to think about how the rest of him must have appeared crushed between van and brick.

He stood up, feeling gravity weigh him down more than ever before. It was difficult to stand. He shook off the awkward sensation and checked his body with his hands for harm. He surveyed the area once again. The black kid had also run out of luck. What was left of his head appeared squished beneath the rear tire, and his intestines were on display for the world to view. The sight made Alejandro vomit, and he wiped his mouth with his sleeve, noticing the driver of the vehicle still lived.

He ran to what remained of the driver's side door and checked over the beaten and bloody body of the man. The survivor tried to move, and Alejandro studied him through the broken window, unsure what to do; he wasn't a first responder. He just worked at a bar. What little Alejandro had learned in the military escaped him.

With shocked amusement, he beheld as the driver pointed a gun at him. Startled, Alejandro took a step back and watched in horror as the driver prepared to shoot with an expression of rage and disgust. A split-second later, life fled the driver's body, and his upper half collapsed face-first into the steering wheel. Joey, like his childhood friend Ricky, was dead.

Alejandro ran. He ran away as fast as he could and kept running until the blaring horn from the driver's dead weight pressing against the steering wheel was well out of earshot.

* * * *

Charles Wethermoore had acquired a disgusting amount of

wealth at a young age. He came into his fortune partly by being born into it and by expanding his inheritance's profitability with savvy ingenuity. Business was in his blood, and he made many decisions, many of which were morally questionable, to gain his current status and power.

Charles despised the many platitudes strewn about to help weaker people feel like they have a chance in life. He lived his life distancing himself from such clichés, but the one about when you want something done right, you must do it yourself raked at the essence of his being. He hated getting his hands dirty, and he loathed the saying because he understood, more often than not, it was true. Cliches carried the burden of coming from a place of truth.

This saying brought Charles to the confusing mess of a south-side neighborhood populated by the people he bled dry. He monitored the young man named Alejandro for a few weeks, and he realized the young man was doing his best to forget the horrible event the local police were clueless about solving.

The driver and passenger of the van were dead; another two vagrant youths died upon the impact of the van smashing into them. A third body was found in a crate in the back of the van. It was a good thing Charles' people retrieved that body when they had, disposing of it in secret. If Charles was right, Alejandro would lead him back to the cargo he lost on that unfortunate mess of a night.

The afternoon sun shined in the sky above, and Charles smirked as Alejandro exited his apartment building and walked along the busy street to the bus stop. He followed young Alejandro and caught up to the youth in no time.

Alejandro sensed someone monitoring him. The events of a few weeks ago left the man paranoid. He turned as a slightly older gentleman - maybe five or six years older than he was - with well-groomed brown hair, and an extravagant tailored suit approached him. The well-dressed stranger smiled and nodded at Alejandro as if they had been old friends, happy to reunite.

"Are you following me?" Alejandro asked.

Charles nodded. "Yes, I am. May I speak to you for a moment?"

Alejandro took a step back. "Who are you?"

"I'm someone who can help you. And in allowing me to help you, you would also help me." Charles smiled again and held out his hand. "My name is Charles Wethermoore."

Alejandro shook the man's hand. "What do you think I can help you with? I don't have a lot of time. I have to get to work."

"I understand. And if you'll indulge me, I assure you that you'll never have to work a dead-end job again. I'm willing to offer a substantial payment for your services in the matter I need to attend to." Charles smiled again. It was a smile used to closing million-dollar deals.

This confused Alejandro. "What do you think I can help you with? I'm nobody special."

Charles shook his head. "You are more skilled than you realize. I have a ship leaving for the Arctic Circle. It's an expedition of sorts. We've found something significant in that area. By us, I mean my team. I've always believed in hand picking the crew for such undertakings. I also take immense pleasure in helping those who deserve it while acquiring their talents. You served in the Navy; is this not correct?"

Alejandro experienced his paranoia growing into fear for his safety. "How do you know so much about me?"

Charles gave him a nonchalant shrug of one accustomed to getting what he wanted. "Your former commander recommended you for this job. Lieutenant Reynolds. He spoke highly of you while I researched candidates for my expedition. I would pay you handsomely, and you'd be a part of something important. World changing. The choice, of course, is yours."

"Why would I go?" Alejandro asked.

A contemplative expression formed on Charles' face. "Because what I'm offering is better than anything you have going on in your life right now. Research me. Do your due diligence. I assure you I am on the level and the type of man who can turn dreams into reality. All I ask in return is for you to be a part of this one job." Charles handed Alejandro a card with information written on the back. "The ship leaves in three days."

Charles turned and began walking away, certain his request would be fulfilled. Alejandro stood somewhat confused at the randomness of the offer, but at the same time, he felt as if this might be his way to the better life he had always dreamed of. What else did he have going for him?

* * * *

Arctic Explorer 1 was a freighter unlike anything Alejandro had ever experienced. The vessel, adorned with reinforced hulls and advanced technology, symbolized the human ingenuity and exploration that Charles Wethermoore's fortune could buy. Its sleek, metallic surface glistened with a coating designed to withstand extreme temperatures and resist the encroachment of ice.

Arctic Explorer 1's deck was a labyrinth of specialized equipment and laboratories, each compartment dedicated to the intricate tasks of the expedition. On the bridge, a team of expert navigators and scientists monitored the ship's progress, their eyes focused on innovative displays designed to relay data from the icy depths below. The freighter was beyond state-of-the-art and anything Alejandro had experienced during his tenure in the United States Navy.

During the voyage, he carried out similar duties that paralleled his life in the military. Still, he also understood anyone with basic sailing knowledge could have carried out the tasks just as well. Charles Wethermoore wanted him for this expedition, and this alone brought Alejandro on board the freighter. He experienced a deep sense of imposter syndrome. Why was he, of all people, here? Sure, he was a sailor, but many other qualified men and women with more experience should have been on this voyage.

As the ship advanced through the Arctic waters, its formidable icebreaker prow led the way, parting the frozen sea with relentless determination. The vessel emitted a low hum as it deployed remotely operated submersibles equipped with the most advanced cameras, sonar, and excavation tools. These robotic explorers dove into the icy abyss, navigating through the murky depths. On deck, Alejandro stared out at the vast Arctic Ocean. The operations fascinated him, and he continued to wonder what motivated a man as rich as Wethermoore to search such a remote area.

As the freighter continued its expedition, it left a trail of ripples on the icy surface, marking the intersection of human curiosity and the enigmatic secrets hidden beneath the Arctic depths. Arctic Explorer 1, a beacon of technological prowess, sailed toward a rendezvous with the unknown. Alejandro wished he understood more but grew fearful that questions might ruin his chances of a better life.

The ship anchored in the middle of nowhere in the deep water of the Arctic Circle. Onboard laboratories buzzed with activity as scientists analyzed data streaming from the submersibles. Excitement and anticipation filled the air. Alejandro wondered at what they discovered. The cold blue liquid surrounded the ship, and, in the distance, patches of ice and glaciers contrasted the water they floated upon. The cold air sent chills up Alejandro's spine as he stood on deck in full Arctic gear. His eyes wandered to a group of individuals congregating at the deck's center.

Four men stood on the main deck, and Alejandro realized they were mercenaries. They were brooding men accustomed to the harshness of war and operated without remorse. The job was all that mattered to them. They appeared capable in matters of combat and were well armed with the latest military-grade weapons and gear thanks to Charles' endless money supply. That he discovered the men's nature long after boarding the freighter left Alejandro with a strong foreboding. When he asked Charles more about the expedition, he was told Charles would reveal the mission details when they reached their destination.

Today, they arrived.

Charles exited the bridge after a brief chat with the captain of Arctic Explorer 1 and walked toward the main deck. He made his way to Alejandro and smiled warmly as he approached. "I hope you're ready for the next phase."

"I didn't realize we were doing this in phases." Alejandro took his eyes away from the ocean's vastness and locked eyes with Charles. "We're in the middle of nowhere. This is where we're stopping?"

Charles nodded. "We've arrived."

Alejandro remained confused. "There's nothing around us."

"Lucky for us, what we're looking for doesn't reside on the surface." Charles winked at Alejandro.

"You found something underwater?" Alejandro felt stupid for not realizing this sooner.

Charles nodded with a grin. "Indeed, we did."

Alejandro sighed. "And you have a sub that can handle the trek?"

"I've spent a small fortune on a cutting-edge submersible vehicle. It can transport us to the proper depth and the location we seek." Charles assured him.

"Why am I here for any of this? You could have hired anybody to do what I'm doing." Alejandro's frustration grew.

"Alejandro, I need you for this. You'll have to have faith in my decision to make you part of the expedition. We found out what's down below in the icy cold depths. We picked up a faint signal, perchance. The odds of discovering it were astronomical - out of this world. We traced the origin of the signal below where we stand." Charles peered down at their feet.

Alejandro grew more curious. "Signal?"

Charles nodded. "We've acquired other items of note. We unearthed one item within the Arctic Circle near Russia. This one carried the same signal."

"I wish you the best heading under." Alejandro moved to attend to more deckhand duties.

Charles reached out and held Alejandro's arm. "I want you to come with us."

Puzzled beyond words, Alejandro averted his gaze from Charles and stared into the ocean. "This makes little sense."

"What doesn't make sense?" Charles took a few steps closer and beheld the majesty of the ocean as well.

"For starters, you want me to go with you below the ocean. You have armed men prepping to head down. Why? Shouldn't you have scientists or something? Men like them," Alejandro pointed, "mean you're expecting some kind of resistance or trouble."

"I promise all will make perfect sense once you head down with us. It's the chance of a lifetime. And those men are a for-mality. They are trained and are here to look after us, nothing more." Charles assured Alejandro again.

Alejandro grunted. He grew more and more curious with each passing second. "When do we head down?"

Charles smiled. "Within the hour."

＊　＊　＊　＊

The name of the submersible provided by Wethermoore's exorbitant wealth was Blue Abyssal. It hovered at the icy surface of the Arctic Ocean, and when the last checks were completed, its streamlined form cut through the frigid waters with a sense of purpose. She was a marvel of modern engineering and boasted a sleek, reinforced hull designed to withstand extreme pressures and navigate the treacherous underwater terrain of the Arctic depths.

The transparent observation dome provided an unparalleled view of the mysterious abyss below, while a suite of advanced sensors and cameras adorned its exterior, ready to capture every detail. The view blew Alejandro's mind. Not once did he expect to go on such a journey. The vehicle's exterior was equipped with bright LED lights, casting an ethereal glow in the otherwise dark depths, adding to the looming sense of mystery pulling on

Alejandro's fears.

The cockpit, illuminated by soft blue light, housed an array of innovative controls and monitors displaying vital information about the submersible's systems and the surrounding environment. The interior remained spacious for a vehicle of its size, and Alejandro stayed seated as instructed. He stole glances at his armed escort, still attempting to determine why they needed the heavy firepower and trained mercenaries. The submersible's thrusters hummed with precision, guiding it toward the designated coordinates, and as they descended, the sinking feeling in Alejandro's stomach that he was in danger increased.

Grady led the four-man team and carried himself with the weight of experience. From the look on his weathered face, one could ascertain he was the kind of man used to making hard decisions in war and could do so again without hesitation. Grady read the information coming through on various instrumentation as Charles made his way to the empty seat next to Alejandro.

"Here we are." Charles smiled again. "Tell me something, Alejandro. Are you familiar with certain Greek mythologies?"

Alejandro kept a watchful eye on the other mercenaries. His senses kept warning him these men were far too dangerous. Doing his best to ease the ill feelings brewing within his gut, he turned to Charles. "Depends on which ones, I guess."

"Hyperboreans come to mind," Charles said.

Grady shot a questioning glance at Charles as he continued to check the instruments of the submersible. Charles returned a superior gaze, reminding Grady he was in charge.

"I'm not familiar with them, I'm afraid," Alejandro answered.

"Well, allow me to tell you." Charles cleared his throat. "They were a people who lived beyond the north wind, or the Boreas, the Greek god of the cold north wind. Legend says it was a magical land. A paradise, where the sun shined without end, and where the people of Hyperborea lived lifespans of a thousand years."

"You're not telling me you think you've found this place, are you?" Alejandro raised a skeptical eyebrow.

Charles gave off a knowing smile. "All myths are formed from basic truths. These two signals are not random. They match and connect to lead us to the truth. Whatever lies beneath the surface is ancient. It predates anything we know. And I truly believe you are a key to helping us gain entrance."

Alejandro failed to stop his nervous laughter. "Gain entrance? What the hell does that mean?"

Charles studied Alejandro with pity. "I apologize for this."

Before Alejandro could say another word, he experienced the sudden impact of a dart in his chest. He gazed upward to the origin of the dart with a hazed vision. Grady grinned with a dart gun in hand.

* * * *

The slow drip of water caused Alejandro's eyes to open. The frigid temperatures added to the discomfort of his wet body, and he sat on a metallic floor that appeared hard on the surface but felt soft. He scanned his surroundings, noticing the open hatch of the submersible and the dripping water from the seal where the vehicle docked. The cold, dark waters of the Arctic circled around the Blue Abyssal submersible and the unknown underwater vessel it attached to. Patterns and symbols that defied Alejandro's understanding dotted the metallic floor as he took in more of his surroundings. After a deep breath, he stood on shaky legs and realized he had a red stain on his shirt. It was blood.

"No...!" The reaction caused Alejandro to take a few steps backward, and in doing so, he tripped on something. While getting his bearings, he focused on his feet and realized he had tripped over Grady's mutilated body; something had maimed Grady almost beyond the point of recognition. While panning the surrounding area, he also recognized the dead bodies of the other team members and of his employer, Charles Wethermoore. They had all been sliced to bits.

The shock of the dead bodies made Alejandro want to run far away, but he soon realized it was a futile gesture. He didn't know how to operate the submersible. Then Alejandro remembered the radio. He might communicate with Arctic Explorer 1 topside. With quickness, Alejandro rushed back inside the Blue Abyssal. To his dismay, the interior of the submersible had been demolished. The instrumentation had been shot to hell by random gunfire, and this included the radio. His only other option was to enter the strange area where he regained consciousness.

Alejandro took a deep breath as he stepped upon the soft metallic substance making up the floor and walls where the vehicle docked. A strange sensation of familiarity overcame him with such power as he took more steps into the underwater entrance. The unknown patterns on the floor lit up, glowing with an alien vibrancy. As the illumination grew, a mysterious hum resonated through the passageway.

He discovered his presence somehow activated the systems of the foreign dwelling. The dark path illuminated further with each step taken, and he followed it, unsure where it would lead. The intricate markings akin to hieroglyphics pulsed and shifted with otherworldly energy. After twisting and turning down a mini labyrinth, he came upon a circular door. More symbols dotted the sides of the sealed entryway. As he stood staring at the barrier, a green light shot from the ceiling, enveloping his entire body. The energy pulsed throughout his system, electrifying every nerve cell. After a few seconds, it disappeared.

The door hissed open as it rolled within a pocket in the wall; a depressurization occurred, and the rattling of old technology rebooting echoed in every direction. Soft, pulsating lights of various hues illuminated the chamber beyond the open door, creating an eerie but mesmerizing ambiance. The metallic material of the unknown ship's interior responded to Alejandro's presence as if alive with alien intelligence.

Alejandro stepped through the opening; the chamber was unusually angular and curved, defying conventional human design principles. The architecture suggested a form of technology and construction that transcended human comprehension. Ethereal energy conduits lined the walls, emitting a soft and soothing light that danced along the edges of the chamber. In the center of the bizarre room were adult-sized pods. He examined the strange substances that made up the pods. The metallic material was alive. One pod had been opened, unlike the rest, which were sealed shut.

The memories came flooding in.

The creatures of this planet were so new and fresh to the creators of what would be known as Hyperborea in legend. The humans needed guidance, and the aliens that built this place and others from off world granted such guidance. They helped to mold humanity and teach humankind during ancient times. The ancient aliens appeared strange. They were knowledgeable, and their feats came across as magic to the primitive human minds worshiping them. This old and powerful race created ME.... This body records all data. It can blend in. It's a machine yet alive.

Alejandro snapped out of his trance with a violent jolt. He yelled in fits of maddened realization while cradling his head.

"This can't be..." His voice sounded strange.

He remembered the night of the car crash. The black van careened out of control. He was hit by the oncoming vehicle and knocked to the side. Fatal wounds resulted from the incident, and help would never have arrived on time. A strange figure appeared above him before he thought his life would end. It didn't have a face, and its skin was silvery from head to toe. The figure held Alejandro and absorbed Alejandro's mind. He remembered carrying his own body and placing it in the empty crate of the van. His actual body died weeks ago. He then blacked out and woke up later near the crash, not recalling any of it.

"I died..." The realization weighed down harder than the depths of the ocean. He studied his hands as he held them before his eyes. "This thing took my form and my memories."

The cryptic speeches Charles gave Alejandro finally made

sense. Alejandro had been the key to this expedition, but some-where along the line, it all backfired. Charles wanted this tech-nology for himself. Such breakthroughs would make an insane profit.

Another memory surfaced. He awoke in the submersible. Grady and the other mercenaries were preparing to exit upon docking. But it wasn't Alejandro who had woken up this time; it was the alien machine that had stolen his soul. His hands be-came razor-sharp claws. Charles and his team of mercs didn't stand a chance. He cut them down within seconds, and despite their training, they were no match for the alien machine.

"I belong here." Alejandro studied the empty pod before him. A sense of being home overwhelmed the man. He laid down in the empty pod and felt the backing mold to his body. The interface linked, and he was one with the ship. *It was wait-ing for me all this time. Now we can leave.*

The pod's cover slid shut, matching the look of the other sealed pods. The green light flashed throughout the room, and the near-silent hum of an alien spacecraft beginning liftoff sent a ripple through the dark waters of the Arctic Circle.

* * * *

The cold ocean waters surrounding the freighter rippled with violent intensity. The captain didn't know what to make of the sudden movement. Any orders for the ship's evasive maneuvers came to him too late. A strange and magnificent vessel rose to the water's surface and sped upward to the sky at such a high speed that it cut through the freighter like the sharpest of blades.

People would wonder for a little while about what happened to the crew of Arctic Explorer 1. No concrete answers would ev-er be found. Conspiracy theories would run wild surrounding the eccentric young billionaire Charles Wethermoore and his final moments. When it was all said and done, she would be another ship lost at sea, along with the truth.

THE WHITE ROOM

STORY 12

COMPLETE DARKNESS SHROUDED Anthony from
the moment of his awakening. A heavy veil of shadows devoured
his surroundings, leaving him with a chilling sense of isolation.
As he attempted to focus his mental faculties, his memory re-
sembled a chaotic jigsaw puzzle, with fragmented images clinging
to the recesses of his mind, much like a distant fog on the horizon, hinting at the ominous secrets lurking beneath.

The darkness enveloping him remained all-encompassing,
suffocating in its intensity, and upon further exploration and self-
examination, he discovered a few unsettling facts that sent shivers
down his spine:

1. His name is Anthony. He clung to this single thread of
identity like a lifeline in this abyss of uncertainty.

2. He was trapped in a room, its dimensions shrouded in this enigmatic void. The walls, invisible but palpable, confined him in a claustrophobic embrace. Every outcome when exploring ended in twenty paces in each direction before hitting an impenetrable barrier.

3. He was clothed, his body free from restraints, yet a gnawing unease whispered that freedom in this Stygian prison might be an illusion.

While pacing about the unfathomable darkness, Anthony toyed with the idea of using his voice to call out for assistance. The ability to speak lived within him, but as he contemplated unleashing his voice into the void, a strange thought gripped him like icy fingers. He couldn't recall ever having spoken before. A sudden wave of dread washed over him, and he dismissed it with haste, attributing it to the fog of his shattered memory.

"Hello?" Anthony's voice broke the oppressive silence, sounding alien and fragile in the engulfing darkness. "Is anyone around? Is anyone listening?"

No response.

"Hello!" Panic coursed through Anthony's veins, his voice pleading. "Can someone please answer me?!" His heart pounded like a drum; his breaths labored as if invisible weights pressed down on his chest. He dropped to his knees, hugging himself in desperation.

A glimmer of hope ignited within Anthony's soul as the vents above him whirred to life, a faint hum cutting through the suffocating silence. In the perceived sounds, he discerned the shifting of panels on the ceiling.

Is this freedom? Am I being released? The questions filled his heart and soul with a fragile sense of joy.

As the ceiling panels ceased moving, Anthony's focus sharpened on the fans within the vents. A sinister hissing, like a serpent on the prowl, descended from above. It melded with the previous noises, weaving an industrial symphony that sent shivers down his spine.

Within seconds, Anthony breathed in the gas seeping into his nasal cavities, a cold, metallic odor invading his senses. Panic surged as realization dawned. He now understood why the fans had been turned on.

A split second later, Anthony's consciousness plunged into the abyss, his world consumed by the pitch-black room, and his fate sealed in chilling obscurity.

* * * *

When Anthony awoke, his eyes struggled to adjust to the sudden harsh light flooding his prison. Four blindingly white walls enclosed him, rendering his sense of direction meaningless. He glanced upward and realized the ceiling was a distant, un-reachable twenty feet above him. The center of the ceiling bore light fixtures and vents, casting an eerie glow.

The haunting notion he had never, in truth, seen before gnawed at him, much like when he found his voice. The intru-sion of light reignited his memories, and they rushed back, vivid and overwhelming. He remembered speaking to people and cherished moments from his past, but his body refused to cor-roborate those recollections.

Anthony examined his hands, noting their soft, delicate tex-ture. His skin possessed an abnormal silkiness, a far cry from the rougher, weathered texture he remembered. He should have a sun-kissed complexion, but it was as if his entire existence had been stripped of its vitality. He also took note of the white cloth-ing clinging to his body, a shade darker than the walls. The cloth-ing, though strange, registered as comfortable on his skin.

"Where am I?" The need to experience his own voice dom-inated his thoughts. "Hello? Where am I? Why am I here? Is my voice reaching anyone?"

Without warning, a seamless, smooth white wall before him

underwent a subtle transformation. A rectangular panel slid without noise on the wall, revealing a tray equal in whiteness, extending toward Anthony. On it, a steaming, soupy meal sat in a white bowl displayed as a piece of culinary art, accompanied by a glass of water.

The aroma of the soup enveloped his senses, a tantalizing scent that beckoned to his insatiable hunger. He scooped the nourishment into his mouth with bare hands, barely pausing to chew as he devoured it with voracious animal instincts. The water followed as a relief that quenched his thirst. Such a simple meal had never left such a divine impression upon his palate. He placed the empty bowl and glass on the tray when he finished.

The tray retreated instantly, sliding back into the wall from whence it came, and the rectangular panel resealed the wall, rendering it solid once more.

A searing explosion of pain erupted within his head as if his mind had been torn open. Anthony attributed the agony to the flood of memories that surged like a tidal wave. Every minute detail of his life unfurled, frame by frame.

"Collins," he whispered through the mental torment. "My last name is Collins." He sank to the ground, rubbing his temples as the anguish subsided with gradual ease. At that moment, a clear image flashed through his mind, vivid and unsettling. "Vanessa." A sad tone dominated his voice.

Vanessa, a beautiful brunette with an insatiable figure to die for, haunted his thoughts. She carried a childlike passion for cotton candy and amusement parks. Her dark brown hair entranced him, and he loved her more than life itself. She was his everything.

The memories of their closeness and intimacy plagued Anthony's mind, sending a shiver down his spine. His body responded to these intense recollections in unsettling ways. A surge of unfamiliar sensations coursed through him, and an uncontrolled reaction surprised him. The erection was sudden and unyielding; his member throbbed with a maddening intensity. His mind recalled the experience in the reservoirs of his memories, but the body seemed to experience it all for the first time.

Lustful thoughts of Vanessa, her beauty, and their shared moments invaded his mind. He remembered the softness of her skin and the passionate kisses they shared. His five senses almost experienced the sensual curves of her voluptuous body, teasing him to act during those most intimate moments. Though he stood alone in the white room, the mind transported the body elsewhere with an imagination more vivid than any reality.

"What's happening to me?" he muttered, his voice laced with confusion.

He stumbled about as if in a drunken stupor.

"Vanessa!" he called out, and a sudden rush of emotion overwhelmed him; the explosive ejaculation lasted only a few seconds, but those precious seconds existed as an eternity's worth of escape from his current situation. The sensation was fleeting, and he ended up with a profound sense of being as lost as when he had awoken in darkness.

As the overwhelming sensation faded, a strange guilt washed over Anthony for the uncontrollable response. He realized these memories held power over him, causing his body to react in unexpected ways. It was maddening, and he hesitated to delve deeper into his recollections, fearing how else his body might betray him.

* * * *

In the sterile confines of his white prison, the only markers of time were the arrival of the meals. Each serving presented a stark variety, shifting from solid substances to soupy porridge, but the water remained a constant, unchanging companion. Anthony's memories teased him with flashes of other beverages — crisp sodas on hot summer days — but they were cruel mirages, dissipating into the monotony of the same stale water served with every meal.

The enigma of how Anthony came to this place persisted as an inscrutable riddle. A mental barrier shrouded a specific memory, concealing it like a shadow in the recesses of his mind. If he could only unveil this hidden knowledge, he believed he might, at last, decipher the purpose behind his eerie confinement. Yet, despite his relentless efforts, the concealed truth remained out of reach with stubborn determination.

* * * *

The pursuit of the elusive memory hidden within Anthony's mind consumed every waking moment. With each passing day, his quest to unravel the enigma slipped further away from his grasp. Isolation, a torment that might have shattered a lesser spirit, instead fueled his determination.

The maddening loneliness and silence that enveloped him could have easily broken him by now. But the missing memory, the one that held the key to his predicament, had become his singular mission. It was the fragile glimmer of hope that sustained him, an obsession that both haunted and preserved his sanity.

* * * *

Frustration couldn't encapsulate the turbulent emotions surging through Anthony's veins. The constant battle to grasp the elusive memory was exasperating beyond measure. When he needed a respite from this fruitless struggle, his thoughts turned to Vanessa. During these moments, a peculiar and overwhelming awareness settled upon him.

He remembered Vanessa in vivid detail, reimagining every nuance and experience stored in his mind. His internal voice served as a haunting narrator, recounting the streaming memories as he relived each moment in his thoughts.

"It was a Thursday, February 21st, 2007," he murmured the thoughts out loud to himself. "Vanessa and I began the day with a senseless argument. We were running late to meet her parents, and I — Anthony, you fool — picked the wrong day for a fight. I was too preoccupied with our heated exchange, not paying attention to the road. I didn't even see the red light."

A flash of the horrific accident raced through Anthony's consciousness. The brutal impact, as their vehicles entangled into a nightmarish mesh of twisted metal, shattered glass, and human suffering, replayed itself with agonizing clarity. He locked eyes with Vanessa as she died, her life extinguished in an instant. The questioning expression on her face of why burned into his mind.

Then, in a chilling revelation, Anthony realized the horrifying truth: on that fateful day, he had died as well.

* * * *

After hours of wallowing in despair, teetering on the brink of complete insanity, Anthony's ears perked up at the faint sound of the rectangular panel sliding open on the smooth white wall. The tray, a familiar presence, advanced towards him as it had done countless times before. However, this time, it greeted him with a chilling deviation from the routine.

Laid out before him was not the usual meal, but a long, razor-sharp silver blade. It gleamed in the sterile light of the white room with ominous undertones.

"What is this?" Anthony's voice trembled as his gaze fixated on the menacing weapon.

In that chilling moment, Anthony experienced Vanessa's voice echoing within the recesses of his mind. *It's your way out, Anthony. Be with me again.*

"It's my way out?" He spoke with a hint of madness; believing he could hear her voice intensified his desperation.

Yes. Use it. Escape the white room.

"Escape..." The idea of escape was so appealing; he just wanted it to end.

Do you love me?

"Of course, I love you." He admitted.

Then do it for me.

With a deep breath, Anthony took hold of the blade and allowed the sharp instrument to pierce the flesh of his abdomen. The pain grew to levels he didn't know he could tolerate, and the blood spilled freely, running across the pristine whiteness of his clothing and the floor beneath him.

"I'll see you soon, Vanessa." The sound of his voice as life left his body made Anthony smile. He was finally free.

* * * *

Calib and Eric stepped into the stark white room where the lifeless power source lay on the ground, its vitality extinguished. The two men were clad in matching black jumpsuits adorned with distinct yellow badges on their left arms, denoting their respective ranks within the company's hierarchy.

These patches served as a silent reminder that Calib and Eric occupied lower rungs on the corporate ladder. It was why they found themselves tasked with the unenviable duty of cleaning up the spent power sources.

Calib, a tall and slender man with a head of dark, almost ebony hair and a Mediterranean complexion, cast a casual glance at the lifeless power source. He shrugged his shoulders with an air of nonchalance.

Beside him, Eric, a younger recruit in the company, monitored Calib's reaction with a mixture of curiosity and apprehension. Eric's short, blond hair and light blue eyes betrayed his newness and nervousness about his role in this operation.

"Is this how it always goes down?" Eric ventured to ask, trying to hide his unease.

Calib shifted his gaze toward Eric, observing the fresh addition to their team as he ran a hand through his short, blond hair. The veteran cleared his throat before responding, "The solitary confinement in the white room is the easiest way to deal with the expired power sources."

Eric frowned; his gaze remained fixed on the lifeless body. "Aren't they just clones in the end?"

Calib gave him a slow nod, understanding the young man's concern. "You could see it that way, but these clones are created from genetic material that's over five hundred years old. The law prohibits cloning from more recent material. Samples have to date back at least five centuries."

"The white room is the easiest way to handle them?" Eric inquired, his voice tinged with sadness.

Calib cleared his throat once again before explaining, "Unfortunately, yes. When a clone in the central power station malfunctions in the stasis pod, it's because they're beginning to recall memories of their life centuries ago. The company tried rehabilitation, but the memories of their death mixed with the awareness of actions they remember performing but never happened in their cloned bodies drove them insane."

"So, there's no alternative," Eric sighed, recalling his first tour of the central power station, with rows upon rows of stasis pods containing these cloned power sources. "All those brains, serving as an organic network."

Calib sensed Eric's distress and spoke reassuringly, "I felt the same way when I first started here. But remember, this plan was put into action during a volatile time in our history. It was a necessary alternative power source. At first, bringing back the dead was frowned upon, but it spared the living from potential extinction. Besides, these subjects have been dead for centuries."

Eric turned to Calib; his gaze appeared troubled. "What if, in five hundred years, you wake up in a room like this?"

Calib shrugged, seemingly unaffected. "I'm the original.

That's a problem my future clone would have to deal with."

LIKE FATHER

STORY 13

"DID YOU WANT another one, Frank?" The older bartender surveyed the dim flickering lights of his dingy establishment as he posed a question to the sole patron seated at the bar. The lights cast dancing shadows across the worn furnishings, and the overall tone of the corner pub screamed mediocrity. The space, while accommodating for a handful of regulars with tales etched in time, remained far from suitable for larger gatherings.

Frank Stevens, at the vibrant age of twenty-five, found solace in the quietude of the establishment. The middle-aged man behind the bar appeared strangely familiar, a fixture in this realm of stories and fleeting moments. As the conversation unfolded over the past hour, Frank couldn't shake the feeling this was more than a chance encounter.

"No thanks, old timer," Frank replied, his gaze studying the lined face of the older keeper of this modest drinking hole. "It's going to be a crazy night for me. I just needed one or two to get the edge off, and they'll ring the alarms if they notice I'm gone. Duty calls."

The cool condensation on the beer bottle served as a fleeting distraction as Frank contemplated the events ahead — the pinnacle of his career, a government-sanctioned experiment, and the audacious pursuit of time travel.

The older bar owner, attentive to the nuances of his patrons, studied Frank's demeanor and couldn't resist prying into the young man's mystery. "So, why would a young man like you feel the need to take the edge off? What could you possibly have going on?" He inquired, deftly removing the empty bottle and wiping the countertop with a damp rag. "Looks like it must be pretty important. I can see the nervousness; you're trying to hide it, but it's coming out."

"It's important, alright. I can't talk about it, though. Don't want to jinx anything." Frank rose from the bar, leaving payment with a generous tip. "Thanks for the drink... Sorry. I didn't catch a name."

"Higgens. Morty Higgens. That's my name, son. Don't you go forgetting now," the old timer smiled, a nod to the transient connections formed in the ebb and flow of time.

"Morty. That's a good name. You take it easy, Morty." Frank stepped into the night with those parting words, leaving the pub behind. The wheels of destiny started turning.

* * * *

"Is everything okay?" Adam directed the question at his life-long friend as they navigated the familiar corridors of the underground facility, a second home where dreams took shape. Their destination, the transport room, held the embodiment of a once-impossible machine, now a tangible reality—a testament to their shared ambition.

Frank thought of the transport room - his life's work. Steel walls adorned with intricate circuitry and flashing control panels surrounded the chamber. In the center stood a futuristic apparatus, the heart of the temporal endeavor. Angular metal arches formed a portal that, when activated, created a shimmering gateway to anywhere in the past. Multicolored lights danced along the edges of the portal, suggesting the manipulation of forces beyond standard comprehension. Only the brightest minds had been enlisted; the government spared no expense in finding scientists from abroad willing to defect for such an endeavor.

"I've never felt better," Frank assured Adam, a confident smile gracing his face. The attire, a throwback to twenty-six years prior, was a deliberate choice for a test run only Frank would undergo. The government-sanctioned experiment teetered on the edge of possibility, and Frank, propelled by youthful exuberance, embraced the unknown.

"I covered for you. Again. I hate it when you sneak out. We're supposed to remain in the facility at all times, especially the night before the damn launch." Adam snickered, clad in a white lab coat that swayed with each step. He couldn't suppress a chuckle as they strolled past coworkers with the necessary security clearance. The camaraderie mirrored their college days, a sense of mischief underlying the gravity of their current endeavor.

Frank acknowledged Adam's cover-up with a knowing grin. "I didn't doubt, for a second, that you wouldn't take care of it. And I knew you'd understand why I needed to escape this claustrophobic underground base and get a little real-world time in before entering the old world." As they continued walking, Frank marveled at the outdated clothing. "Can you believe people dressed like this?"

"Yes, I can, but that's not what concerns me right now," Adam confessed.

"What's bothering you?" Frank inquired, his nerves beginning to act up.

"You know the government has a ton of willing volunteers

willing to go into the transport room, no questions asked. You don't have to be the one to go this time around." Adam's concern was palpable.

Frank gently but firmly gripped Adam's shoulders. "There's no way in hell I'll let anyone else do this before me. The probes we sent back checked out, and they returned intact. This is the next logical step, Adam."

Adam sighed. "Probes are one thing. A human person is another story. And I don't know if I can keep this up when you're gone. What if something goes wrong? What if you get stuck there?"

"Then I'll take the long way around." Frank smiled. "You got this."

"I'm not so sure," Adam admitted.

Frank locked eyes with his lifelong friend. "You understand what they need to make this machine work. The two of us came up with this thing together, remember? And you, my friend, are more the brains than I am. You led the best team of scientists in the world to get to this moment. You did! I'm just the salesman who helped get us here and a grunt with some test piloting experience. And this opportunity to go back is my part in all of this. I've been training for it."

"You're not selling me right now," Adam admitted.

"I'm telling you, Adam, that there is absolutely nothing to worry about." Frank exuded confidence that began dissipating.

"Famous last words, huh?" Adam eyed Frank.

"Now, why do you have to go and say some shit like that?" Frank winked at his friend before progressing through the final checkpoints, where military guards verified his identification. "I'll see you when I get back, Adam."

Adam's determined nod was the last exchange of looks between friends before he swiftly moved to his post in the control room, eager to be a part of the historic moment unfolding. Deep within, Adam understood with certainty that the control room held the crucible of decision-making, crucial for Frank's survival in the first documented travel through time.

The control room buzzed with activity as techs dashed between stations, conducting last-minute diagnostics and ensuring the seamless operation of all systems. Adam, overseeing every detail, made rounds, addressed queries, and checked on specific tasks. Monitors displayed complex algorithms and calculations, a digital symphony orchestrating the delicate dance of temporal manipulation. Technicians in white lab coats moved purposefully between stations, overseeing the last-minute preparations with an air of anticipation. Satisfied, he took his seat at the primary station, embodying the role of a captain embarking on a new vessel. A deep, relaxing breath signaled his readiness.

"Listen up, people. This project was a long time coming. Let's make sure we do it right," Adam declared, donning his headset and focusing on the main screen. Frank stood isolated in the travel chamber, eager for the momentous departure.

"Come on, Adam, let's get this show on the road already," Frank's voice resonated in the headset.

"Take it easy. Stay calm, and don't move. We've initiated the sequence, and it needs to capture you as you are," Adam explained.

An explosion at the entrance shattered the steel doors and the anticipated moment of glory. Armed troops dressed in unfamiliar military uniforms stormed the control room, firing upon techs who attempted to resist. A hostile force invaded the base and breached every inch of the complex.

"What is this? Who are you?" Adam stood, fear coursing through him as he realized he needed to take control of the situation.

"Adam? What's going on out there, man?" Frank's voice inquired through the earpiece. On the main screen, Frank paced anxiously in the travel chamber, eager to assist his friend. *"I don't like what I'm hearing on my end, buddy. What the hell is going on?"*

Before Adam could respond, a gunshot echoed through the room. He toppled over the console, wounded and frightened. He understood his lifelong friend only had one way out of this nightmare. With a hand dripping in blood from holding his wounded stomach, Adam reached for the activation button and prayed Frank would end up in a safe place and time. The control room, once a realm of dreams, now bore witness to the tragedy that unfolded in the name of scientific progress.

* * * *

Nicole Agna was caught at the crossroads of disbelief and compassion as the strange man materialized before her. Shock paralyzed her initial reaction, making the prospect of involving authorities or seeking medical help seem far-fetched. The tale she would have to tell, of a man appearing out of nowhere, bordered on the surreal, and she hesitated to be labeled as someone who believed in the impossible.

Despite her uncertainties, Nicole, a certified nurse, recognized the superficial wounds adorning the stranger's body. Logic dictated that, with time and care, he would regain consciousness. Trusting her instincts, she brought him to her home, a farmhouse on the outskirts of a small Midwestern town. Isolated, with no other living soul for miles, her abode became an unexpected sanctuary for a man she couldn't ignore. Half a day passed in vigilant care as she tended to the stranger's needs, an odd connection forming between them. The typically serene farmhouse now harbored the enigmatic presence of a man who materialized out of thin air.

As he awoke, Frank stretched in a manner reminiscent of any ordinary morning in his apartment. The realization hit him — the project succeeded, catapulting him roughly twenty-six years into the past.

"It's okay. I found you on the side of the road and brought you here. You're lucky I was passing by, too. There isn't anyone around these parts for miles," Nicole explained, her voice a blend of concern and curiosity.

Surveying the bandages around his arms and ribs, Frank questioned, "What happened to me?"

"You experienced some minor skin tearing, like rips or cuts. I cleaned the wounds while you slept. They were all superficial. I have no idea how you got the cuts, though. You kind of appeared out of nowhere. Those cuts are strange. Maybe you could shed some light on how you got them." Her gaze grew intense. She needed this to make sense.

Frank rubbed his head, grappling with the disorientation that accompanied time travel. Adam, you bastard. You saved my life. The thought lingered. "I'm guessing it resulted from the travel," he admitted, uncertain how much to reveal to this woman who unwittingly became a part of his temporal odyssey.

"I don't follow. What kind of travel are you talking about?" Nicole's smile radiated simplicity and beauty as she tucked her shoulder-length light brown hair behind her ears. "You okay? Physically, you are, but I mean..." She pointed to her head.

Frank sat up, bringing himself to Nicole's eye level as she sat beside him. "I'm okay, I mean it. Did I have anything with me when you found me?"

"Just the clothes on your back." She stood from the bed, walking to the dresser, where a tray with food and water awaited. "Lucky you're dealing with a farm girl, mister. I had to shove you in my car all by myself. You're heavy."

"Of course, they didn't have time to give me the device for return." Frank rubbed his head, ignoring her last comment and feeling a hangover multiplied by ten. He graciously took the tray from Nicole, gulping down water with a realization of his intense thirst. Setting the tray aside, he studied Nicole as she sat beside him again, preparing to gauge her reaction to what he was about to ask. "This will sound like a crazy question, but what year is it?"

"2024. And believe me, I've been asked crazier." She smiled.

"I didn't catch your name," Frank noted her beauty for the first time.

Still smiling, she said: "Nicole. Nicole Agna."

"Strange sounding last name you got there. But I like it. It's nice." Frank allowed himself to smile this time.

"I guess I'll take that as a compliment. What do you go by? Or did you forget your name along with the year?" She smirked.

Frank recalled an old-timer's name from a friendly drink when contemplating the ramifications of revealing too much. "My name is Morty Higgens."

She raised an eyebrow. "I wouldn't go around telling people their name is strange sounding when you have a name like Morty. It's a pleasure to make your acquaintance, Morty. Do you need to call anyone?"

"No. I've got nobody and literally no place to go. And I thank you for your help. I'll be on my way. I've troubled you enough, and you've already done more than most would." Frank attempted to rise from the bed.

"Don't be silly. If you're as bad up for luck as you say, I'll feel guilty for not helping you out, especially if something ill comes of it." She stood from the side of the bed. "Eat up. You'll need your strength. Tomorrow, we'll get you some decent clothes, and after that, we'll take it one step at a time. Then you can do whatever you think you need to." She nodded in approval to herself. She felt comfortable around Morty. Deep down, she sensed she could trust him.

"Thank you." Frank smiled, experiencing an ineffable connection. "I appreciate your help, Nicole."

"The pleasure is all mine, Morty Higgens." She smiled as she exited the room.

Frank lay down on the bed, allowing the shock of his current situation to sink in with a full-blown panic attack. The attack took hold of his chest the instant Nicole left the bedroom, and he curled deep into the bed, breathing slowly, allowing his body to adjust. Eventually, he forced himself to get used to the idea that this was now his reality. He would have to take the long way around to get home.

* * * *

Having been raised as a city boy, Frank had no idea about the greatness rural life afforded. Nicole's humble estate was rustic in every sense of the word. It was farmland with nothing to farm, and the house was large enough to always have something that needed fixing. The constant maintenance and work to support them kept Frank (or Morty) rather busy. He arrived out of thin air over a year ago, and he and Nicole would soon bring their baby into the world. Frank had grown so accustomed to the name Morty that he nearly forgot who Frank Stevens had been.

False papers under the identity of Morty Higgens were easy enough to come by. He would sneak off behind Nicole's back to obtain the proper documentation and get the identity in order. Once he ironed out the details, he made a life for himself and Nicole in their secluded piece of heaven. At times, he would think of Adam and what once was, but during most moments, he kept himself grounded in the present (or his past, depending on perspective). Given his circumstances, he remained sane by rooting himself here and now.

While working out in the field, tending to the massive lawn in constant need of attention, Nicole stood at the doorway of their home. She searched with her eyes, spotting Morty in the field fumbling with a riding lawn mower not worth the trouble. She screamed at the top of her lungs, "My water broke, you bastard! Take me to the hospital!"

Dumbfounded at first but filled with elation, Morty ran to his lover, took her by the hand, and led her to the car. Morty was about to be a father for the first time, which excited the man to no end. Their secluded life was about to welcome a new member, a joyous continuation of the strange and unexpected journey that began with a man appearing out of thin air.

* * * *

"Which one is yours?" An older gentleman in a black suit asked while standing beside Morty in the hospital corridor. His features were hard, and he struck Morty like the last person you would expect to find in a hospital viewing the newborns.

"That one is mine. The one the nurse just put into the crib." So overjoyed at being a father, Morty failed to recognize the man's strange demeanor. But in the back of Frank's trained mind, he sensed something wasn't right. "What about you?"

"I'm still waiting to see. Congratulations." The man in black turned to face Frank. "I'm Sal." He extended his hand.

"Morty." Frank took it, feeling the calloused roughness of Sal's tight grip.

"Morty?" Sal laughed. "That's a hell of a name. Your parents actually named you that?"

Frank shrugged. "What they lacked in creativity, they made up for with love."

Sal smirked at the comment. "You're a quick one." The rough man turned his gaze through the window. His gaze appeared laser-focused on Morty's son. "Make sure you take care of your boy there. Good fathers are scarce."

This disturbed Frank. His physical demeanor remained calm even though his instincts signaled fight or flight. "Speaking from experience there, Sal?" Frank lifted his hands in an apologetic gesture. "I don't mean to pry. Sorry about that. Sometimes, the words come out of my mouth before I realize what I'm saying."

"No need to worry, Morty. No need to worry at all. My dad was a genuine piece of work. I just hate to see history repeat itself. Know what I mean?" Sal stood tall, cracked his neck, and patted Frank on the shoulder. "Take care."

"You too." Frank didn't know what else to say.

Sal turned and sauntered off, moving with glacial speed away from the neonatal nursery.

Bothered by the strange encounter, Frank became compelled to check in on the mother of his child. He rushed down the hallway of the hospital and entered her recovery room to find her eyes filled with tears of fright.

Without hesitation, he ran to her, holding her close. "Hey, now, what's the matter? This is a happy time. You shouldn't be crying like this."

"Morty, there's something I need to tell you. Something I couldn't tell you before." In a panicked state, Nicole seemed relieved to have Morty enter the room.

"What is it?" Morty asked, confused.

With heavy eyes, Nicole locked eyes with the love of her life, gently running her fingers through his hair. "I'm not who you think I am. My real name isn't Nicole Agna. It's a fake one I've been living under. I've been in hiding for quite some time now."

"What are you talking about?" Frank's confusion grew. His old self returned to the surface, usurping Morty's carefully crafted identity.

Her frantic nature kept pace with every word. "Remember how you said you didn't like to talk about your past? You left it at that you were adopted and didn't really know your parents? Well, this was something I kept to myself, but I can't do it anymore because they found me. I wanted to tell you but didn't want to scare you away. They're going to kill me now that they know where I am. We need to get our baby and get out of here as fast as we can!"

Morty failed to understand. "Nicole, let's calm-"

"-Nicole isn't my real name!" She interrupted.

Frank stood from the bed, looking Nicole in the eye, trying to wrap his mind around the strange revelation. "What's your real name?"

"Evalyn Stevens." She admitted.

The shock of the name slammed into Frank's chest like a sledgehammer. He stood, unable to move or utter a sound. Frank Stevens gazed at the woman he loved, piecing together the terrifying truth that flashed through his mind like blaring sirens. "No... It can't be true..."

"Honey, now is not the time to panic. We have to get our

baby out of here right now." She reached out to him from the hospital bed.

This can't be possible! I was Frank! I am Frank! That child in there is Frank Mackie, and he'll become Frank Stevens! My birth mother's name was Evalyn Stevens.... When I found out, I took her last name and got rid of my adopted name, Mackie. Frank Mackie! That's my child, but that's me at the same time! It can't be possible!

Confusion set in as Frank stumbled about the recovery room, drunk by the influx of earth-shattering information. He nearly forgot his lover was lying on the bed across from him while a dizzying nature occupied his senses. He could barely keep track of anything in the room, finding it incredibly difficult to focus. That was his lover; that was his mother.

"Morty!" Nicole did her best to sit up on the bed. "We have to get out of here! I saw him, and he knows I did! He's waiting for the right time to kill me. Did you hear me? He wants me dead, and if we don't get out of here right now, that's exactly what will happen!"

"We have to call the cops." Frank did his best to maintain his sanity while trying to gather her things in the recovery room.

"No! The cops want me too! I've been hiding from all of them. You're all I've got, Morty. You're all I need. I need you to trust me and go do what I ask. Go get our baby, and then we can all get out of here." She pleaded with him.

Understanding his timeline and knowing the inevitable outcome of this situation, Frank studied Nicole with heavy eyes. He was adopted. He would never know his mother or father. "What did you do?"

She shook the question away with an exasperated gesture. "That doesn't matter anymore. What matters now is getting out of here. Go get our baby." Nicole wiped away more frantic tears. "He has your face. Our boy has his father's face."

"I love you," Frank said, experiencing a mixture of adoration and disgust.

"I love you too. Now go!" Her voice never sounded so desperate.

Frank bolted from the recovery room and stood outside of the nursery where the baby - where he - was crying. At that moment, a flat line rang through the hospital, broadcasting from Nicole's recovery room. Nursing staff on hand entered to ascertain and quickly respond to the emergency. They would infer it had been because of complications from the birth.

It was supposed to be this way. Frank mentally repeated this sentence in his mind over and over. *I'm my own father!* He took a step back, barely able to contain the vomit that fought to push its way up from the bowels of his stomach.

While taking slow, steady steps to leave the hospital, Frank glimpsed the man dressed in black from the corner of his eye. He put together who the cause of Nicole's death was, and with volatile hatred, he monitored as Sal exited the floor through a stairwell.

At least I can make something right from all of this. With a newfound determination, Frank embarked on a mission to confront the man in black, seeking justice for Nicole and the child that was, in a perplexing twist, his own past self.

* * * *

The exit to the stairwell led straight to the back of the hospital, where a parked car waited for Sal. Not another soul existed in the area designated for medical waste pickup, and the man in the black suit was confident of this. He planned his exit strategy with care.

Many years ago, Evalyn Stevens ran the books for Sal's boss. The organization had its hands in every operation conceivable. She kept track of the ins and outs of every dollar. Over time, she began skimming off the top and ran off with a sizable sum. Finding the woman presented its share of challenges, but Sal finally caught up to her. Evalyn Stevens was now dead. Sal's boss would be happy.

The sudden impact of a metal bar on the side of Sal's head didn't give him time to react or even see who attacked him. All he could hear as the blunt instrument smashed violently into his skull over and over was an angry chant.

"This is for Evalyn! This is for Evalyn!" The rage in Frank's voice spurred him on to deeper levels of violence.

Eventually, there was nothing. The pain led to complete darkness. Sal was dead.

Frank stood over the lifeless body, a mix of relief and rage coursing through his veins. He focused on the moment and checked the body for the key fab to the car.

I have to disappear, Frank thought.

He wiped the blood from his hands and entered the black sedan. The car started on the first try, and he fled the hospital, leaving himself behind.

*   *   *   *

"I certainly look like an old-timer," Morty Higgens thought while surveying his empty corner bar. No one had been in for a drink in hours, and Morty studied the clock on the wall, having waited nearly twenty-five years for this coming moment to unfold.

The front door of the corner pub opened, and a young man entered casually, studying Morty's establishment. The young man appeared on edge as if about to embark upon something dangerous. "This sure is a nice place you got here, old-timer. I don't think I've ever had the pleasure of coming here before now."

"It pays the bills," Morty smirked. "I'm willing to bet you'll be having a cold beer. A pale ale, perhaps? Am I right?"

"How do you know I wouldn't want a fancy mixed drink?" The young man suggested, testing the waters.

Morty scoffed. "Cause a beer is what I would've asked for. Have a seat. Looks like you need to take the edge off."

"You call them like you see them. I'll have a seat and your finest pale ale in a bottle." Frank Stevens smiled, looking at the old man as he approached the bar. There was something familiar about the bartender Frank couldn't quite shake. "My name is Frank. Frank Stevens. A pleasure to meet you."

"Believe me, son, when I say the pleasure is mine." The air in the bar charged with a strange energy, as if the past and present converged in this seemingly ordinary corner pub.

* * * *

He made it, Adam thought, clinging on to the last bit of life remaining within him. The invading troops had ransacked the facility, stealing vital hard drives and critical components to the transport room.

The wound hurt and felt numb at the same time. The blood covered Adam's white lab coat, and he surveyed the other techs in the control room. They were all dead save him. He understood he wouldn't be alive for much longer.

In the throws of what he considered to be a hallucination, Adam witnessed an older man walk through the blasted steel door. The older man looked at the room with recognition as if he hadn't laid his eyes on it in decades.

"I would have been here sooner, but I had to take the long way around." Frank smiled at his lifelong friend.

"No..." Adam coughed, blood trickled from his mouth.

Frank walked to Adam's side and kneeled down. He carried a medkit in his hands. The technology was state-of-the-art and used for soldiers on the field with wounds like the one Adam sustained.

"Frank?" Adam touched the older face. "You got old."

"Happens to everyone," Frank admitted. "Your machine

works." He attached the portable medkit to Adam's abdomen. "And I can't let you die. I wouldn't. I've been waiting to come here for twenty-six years."

"How did you get in?" Adam asked, feeling the effects of the medkit at work. The Smart machine checked his vitals and administered the proper aid. Nanotech dealt with the bullet, working to remove the foreign object.

"I'm an old bastard now, but the biosecurity still recognizes me as me." He helped Adam to his feet.

"Anyone else alive?" Adam looked over the dead technicians one more time.

"A few made it to the secure panic room." Frank led his friend to the destroyed entrance.

"You saved me." Adam's emotions got the better of him. Tears formed.

"You saved me first." Frank nodded, granting his friend a reassuring smile.

"Who attacked us?" Adam asked as they exited the control room to rendezvous with the other survivors.

"We have plenty of time to figure that out," Frank assured him. "As much time as we need."

THE MANY LIVES OF AKIRREL

STORY 14

THE CADENCE OF the two warriors echoed through the dry desert air as blades clashed, leaving the impression of a beautiful yet violent dance. It ended as soon as it began; Akirrel once again became the victor. Another lifeless body lay before him, and another faceless soul fool enough to battle one of the Never Enders discovered the eternal dream. The nameless swordsman now joined the ranks of countless mortals who defied those who can never die.

The badlands beyond the mountain castle of Grebde stretched for miles, a desolate landscape reaching the outer edges of Akirrel's ancient eyesight; he recalled when this wasteland once housed a variety of life. This happened eons ago. In the now rugged desert terrain, Akirrel mounted his black stallion, a faithful companion and war horse used to the chaos of battle. At a steady pace, he galloped past the fallen foe, traversing the expansive desert landscape on a journey to meet his fate.

The black horse stirred with unease, coming to a sudden halt. Its senses detected something unnoticed by the warrior riding him. In a split second, the desert sands cracked and broke for miles, shaking with violent intensity. On both sides of the Never Ender, two human figures shot forth, spewing the cracked landscape of the badlands in every direction as they erupted from the ground. The two mysterious figures flipped overhead of Akirrel with swords drawn, ready to attack. Akirrel bent backward, maneuvering with quick grace, narrowly evading a slice directed at his head. Simultaneously, he unsheathed his sword, blocking the second figure's deadly blow aimed at him. The two men landed on opposite sides with feline grace.

Never Enders like me! Akirrel exclaimed in his mind. Shock filled him as he realized two of his own kind worked together. Most Never Enders avoided each other or tried to eliminate one another. Immortal through reincarnation, they retained memories and experiences of previous lives. Over their eons of existence, the sins Never Enders carried out against one another remained beyond measure.

"The badlands are no place for others like us," one of the men, covered in cracked dirt, remarked, shaking off the sand. "What brings you to our domain?"

"Your domain, is it?" Akirrel smirked, holding back laughter. "What makes you think lands such as these belong to you? The harsh realm named the badlands belongs only to death."

"It appears you're in luck, for death is who you've found on this day," the second man declared, soaring through the air toward Akirrel.

Akirrel dismounted the stallion with ease, skillfully blocking the flurry of blows. The second figure, quick and precise, attacked with obliviousness regarding Akirrel's identity; Akirrel was one of the oldest and most experienced among the Never Enders.

Having tested his opponent, Akirrel sheathed his sword with the grace of experience, dodging thrusts and slices from various angles. He stood his ground for a few more heartbeats and frustrated his opponent further by disarming him and holding the sword to his neck.

"Release him!" the first man shouted.

"Who are you two to be working together in such a manner? Feuding to our kind comes as natural as breathing," Akirrel stated, his gaze fixed on the captive. "And you, my friend, require a few more lifetimes' worth of practice."

Nimaj'neb lowered his head in a respectful bow. "His name is Otos. I go by Nimaj'neb. Your skill is beyond impressive, and it is clear we are not your equals. I beg you to be kind and allow my brother more time before you force him to be born again." As he spoke, Nimaj'neb sheathed his sword, acknowledging the undeniable prowess of Akirrel.

Outraged, Otos shot a scowl at his brother. "How dare you grovel before this swine? Luck guided his hand on this day!"

"He disarmed you, brother! Let it be!" Nimaj'neb rose slowly, his gaze now fixed on the man who held his brother's life in his hands. He regarded Akirrel's tailored red clothing, reminiscent of a time long past. "You ride a mighty horse. It's a miracle you managed to maintain its life across these harsh lands."

"When you have lived again and again as I have, you learn quite a bit regarding survival." Akirrel stepped to the side with lightning-quick speed and returned the sword to Otos' sheath. Afterward, he ambled to the black stallion, who waited for his master with eagerness. "My name is Akirrel, in lives past and in this one."

Amazed, Otos bowed his head and fell to his knees. "You're one of the First! Forgive me, Master Akirrel!"

"We owe a debt!" Nimaj'neb bowed deeper than his brother. "You spared my brother a premature reincarnation. We serve you until the debt is repaid in full, no matter how many lifetimes it may take."

While mounting his stallion, Akirrel gazed down at the two brothers. "I've no need of servants, and no debt stands between us. You two are free, as you've always been."

"We are honor-bound. You would wound us by denying it,"

Otos declared. He stood before Akirrel, ready to defend in order to prove his fealty.

With two Never Enders on my side, I may defeat him. Elyk will pay for his treachery, as will Maya. I possess the secret, and the Never Enders will be reincarnated no more, only to meet the true death. These two will be useful. A smile formed on Akirrel's face as he regarded the now loyal subjects. The surrounding air charged with a newfound sense of purpose, and the vibrant loyalty of the brothers added dynamic energy to Akirrel's unfolding saga.

* * * *

"Lerrika, honey, what are you doing now?" Sanda asked as she opened the sliding door to her daughter's room. The colony withstood much hardship on the distant planet of Iltej, and Sanda faced a multitude of challenging tasks as the Chief Environmental Engineer. The room, although small, reflected a blend of smart devices controlled through voice and mind commands. The AI assistant designated to Sanda's home stayed linked to the robotic helpers designed to alleviate some of the challenges faced by the colonists. Those robots kept Lerrika's room clean. Although they lived on another planet forging a new society for humanity, a teenager's room remained a teenager's room.

"Mother, please! I've asked you before to announce yourself before entering my room!" Lerrika pouted, surrounded by holographic displays and a sleek computer setup that responded to Lerrika's every word. As of late, the rift between mother and daughter widened. Lerrika fought for independence, while Sanda sought only to protect her only child in the unforgiving environment of Iltej.

"I'm sorry, honey. Supper is ready, and your father and I grew curious about what you've been doing up here." Like most mothers, Sanda picked up the stray clothing lying about Lerrika's room, assisting the robotic clean-up crew. "It wouldn't hurt you to stay a bit on the tidy side of things." The robots appeared to agree with a series of beeps.

"And it wouldn't hurt you to stop being nosy. If you must know, I'm working on a story." She turned around on the swivel chair that molded to her body, creating the perfect ergonomic experience. She pointed with pride at the computer display. No keyboard was necessary since all her thoughts were transmitted to the computer via the wireless chip implanted at birth. Every colony person wore one to locate those lost in the harsher terrains and communicate and link them with life-saving equipment. They also served to activate and direct everyday amenities in the home.

Sanda smiled. "We have a budding author in the family. I believe this makes you the first. May I read some of it?"

"Not yet, Mother. It isn't finished. But when I finish, it'll be grand!" The enthusiasm welled up inside Lerrika so much that she felt herself on the verge of an emotional explosion.

"Of this, I have no doubt, my darling daughter." Sanda planted a quick kiss on her daughter's forehead and laughed as Lerrika wiped it away.

"I hate it when you do that, Mother," Lerrika complained.

"But I love the way you react when I do." Sanda smiled. "Now, before we go down and eat dinner, can you at least tell me the name of this novel?"

Lerrika beamed with joy. "The title will be The Many Lives of Akirrel. I've named it after the protagonist."

Sanda raised an eyebrow in curiosity. "And what is this Akirrel like, my darling daughter?"

She closed her eyes, imagining her creation. "For starters, he's handsome. He has long, shimmering black hair that he puts back in a ponytail, and he's the best swordsman around. Elyk is better, though, and Elyk is his mortal enemy. Did I mention the part about reincarnation?"

Sanda shook her head from side to side and smiled as mothers do.

"Oh, that's the best part! It's what makes the story!" Lerrika cleared her throat before she continued. "The people in the story are what I call Never Enders. They keep all the memories and experiences of their previous lives and have, therefore, died and lived time and time again, moving from body to body with every generation. In a way, they are immortal and trapped in their world, watching it change with time. They can't move on to the next world after death."

"Sounds fascinating!" Sanda smiled. "I can't wait to read it."

Lerrika bobbed her head with approval. "I can't wait to finish it. Shall we head down, Mother?"

Sanda nodded. "Yes, we shall."

Both mother and daughter stood up and exited Lerrika's bedroom. Sanda led the way down the stairs and into the kitchen, where Lerrika's father, Danjo, awaited to feast on the meal prepared by the food sequencer. The device was a perk of being the Chief Environment Engineer and was delivered during a recent shipment from Mother World.

Lerrika sighed as she moved down the stairs behind her mother. It frustrated her to stop what she was doing, but the story would have to wait. The ambient hum of the technology in their colony house and the distant sounds of life on Iltej through open windows surrounded them as they descended, creating a backdrop for the intertwined lives of a family living in a distant and challenging world.

* * * *

Storming the castle remained the easier part of the plan. The troops raised by Akirrel followed him to the death; he stood as their personal messiah, and they became his ordained people, chosen for this purpose. Akirrel used their fanaticism as a means to an end, and they fought and died, utilizing the blood of the slain as a symbol of their salvation. The disruption created by the small army worked as intended. Akirrel and his fellow Never Enders entered the mountain castle of Grebde amid the chaos. Vengeance would be theirs.

Otos and Nimaj'neb maintained a vigilant eye as they crept through the open chamber where Maya and Elyk would be found. The earth tones that made Otos and Nimaj'neb blend in while living in the badlands did nothing to camouflage them as they stalked through the decorated chamber, which housed elaborate artwork from all over the kingdom. Akirrel wore white, the color of purity. His clothing was covered in the blood of those sacrificed for his glory, and the white faded into varying shades of the red stain.

The chamber, adorned with intricate carvings and tapestries, resonated with an air of ancient power and dark history. Torches flickered, casting dancing shadows on the walls as if the essence of the place was alive with malevolence. Otos and Nimaj'neb moved with stealth, their footsteps creating a faint echo against the cold stone floor.

"How many times must I kill you, Akirrel?" Elyk stepped from behind one of the massive pillars in the chamber. He stood in a suit of golden armor; his silver hair was tucked beneath the helmet. Elyk carried his sword in hand.

Akirrel smirked. "It won't be a concern for much longer. I discovered magic capable of putting a stop to our reincarnations. I will use it on you the moment my sword pierces your flesh, and you shall be reborn no more."

"We shall see, Akirrel. As for your companions, well, they have their own demons to battle." With the wave of a hand, two shadowy figures appeared before Otos and Nimaj'neb. The life-less shadows formed into versions of the two warriors and opened their dark eyes in unison.

The shadows cast eerie reflections on the chamber walls, creating an atmosphere of impending doom. "What evil is this?!" Otos cried, sword in hand and ready to fight.

"You have defeated many when entering this castle. Let's see how well you do against your very self." Elyk wasted no time charging Akirrel as the shadow copies attacked their counter-parts with deadly precision.

Akirrel fought the battle of his life, deflecting blow after blow made upon him by Elyk. From his peripheral, Akirrel spotted Maya watching the fight unfold. She lay atop a long bed placed in the center of the chamber. The green silk dress fit her curvy body like a second skin, and the image of her beauty was enough to bring Akirrel to his knees.

"She is mine, Akirrel! This has always been the case!" Elyk's voice boomed as his relentless attack continued.

The air crackled with tension as the clash of swords echoed through the chamber. The torchlight flickered in rhythm with the intense duel, casting dynamic shadows that danced along the ancient walls.

I must gain the upper hand! Akirrel summoned all his strength.

Otos struggled with himself literally while dueling with his shadow copy. The dark counterpart expected his actions before he took them, and the appropriate counters met each attack Otos attempted. He kept a watchful gaze on Nimaj'neb as they fought. "We cannot continue like this, Nimaj'neb."

"I agree, brother." Nimaj'neb fought his dark counterpart, finding the same difficulties. "I'm aware of your weaknesses."

Otos smirked. "And I yours."

"Then we shall see who the better swordsman is!" Nimaj'neb bellowed.

With the ease of a leaf floating upon a gentle wind, the brothers switched opponents so they would face each other's shadow copies. This threw the dark counterparts off, as they failed to anticipate the attacks made against them by the duo. Working together, the two brothers made quick work of their dark rivals, striking each down simultaneously. When finished, they cast their gaze upon Akirrel, who continued to struggle with Elyk.

"We must help him!" Otos grew angry to discover his broth-er's hand holding him back.

"We must not take action." Nimaj'neb beheld Akirrel's battle. "This is his fight. He must do this on his own. Our debt has been repaid tenfold with the storming of this castle alone, not to mention our previous exploits with one of the First. Whether he survives depends upon his will."

The two brothers glanced at the beautiful Maya. She lay like a goddess, her golden hair dancing in the breeze sweeping through the chamber. The open balcony peering down to the mountain's base was good for such things.

"She is the root cause of all of this." Otos wanted nothing more than to pierce his sword through her flesh. He felt the demon beneath the mask of beauty as she eyed him from where she lay.

"That she is, my brother. That she is." Nimaj'neb agreed.

Maya took her eyes off the two, knowing they posed a minor threat to her. Instead, she focused on Akirrel and Elyk as they battled throughout the massive chamber, showing no mercy with their intense movements.

I've lost count of how many times I've witnessed these two do battle. I can't remember the first time. Her memory was vast, and she struggled to recover specific experiences from her past.

"In all these lives, have you learned nothing?" Elyk struck down hard and sidestepped a slice, moving in. His sword slashed along Akirrel's abdomen as he passed by.

Akirrel gazed down. He saw his own blood soaking through the white clothing he wore and lost track of it as it mixed with the blood of his enemies. The white that remained on his clothing was sporadic.

Elyk waited with patience for Akirrel's next move. "You're going to die again, Akirrel."

"No!" Akirrel charged Elyk with the strength and force of an army. His barrage of slices and thrusts would have been a series of blurs to the naked eye. His superhuman effort became relentless. "You will die!"

Surprised by the sudden onslaught, Elyk struggled to block each blow made against him. They danced the dance of death as they moved throughout the chamber. Maya watched and waited; the brothers did the same. Without warning, Elyk smiled and, with a free hand, summoned a bit of the magic he had gathered over his many lives.

The ground in the chamber shook around Otos and Nimaj'neb. The chamber, once a grand display of opulence, now manifested its malevolent power as the structure rebelled against the intruders. Hands and arms made of the marble floor reached out and held the two brothers in place. The hands of stone tightened their grip on Otos and Nimaj'neb, creating an ethereal prison that resonated with the echoes of ancient curses. They yelled in fury at their sudden imprisonment.

Another hand and arm emerged from the marble behind Akirrel as he blocked strikes against him with his sword. The red and gold marble of the chamber floor lifted high in the air, re-sembling a giant serpent ready to strike. The fingers flexed with fury as the hand seized Akirrel, forcing him to drop his sword with an intense grip that enveloped his entire body. The Never Ender found it impossible to breathe, the weight of the magical imprisonment pressing down on him.

Unable to hide his satisfaction, Elyk laughed, allowing his devilish smile to grow from ear to ear. He walked to Akirrel with golden armor shining and sword in hand. "You've fought well but will never be good enough to defeat me, Akirrel."

"I'll return, Elyk. No matter how often death takes me from this realm, I will return and have my vengeance!" Akirrel strug-gled with the marble hand holding him in place. His rage kept him from noticing the wound in his abdomen bleeding out and opening up as the deadly grip grew tighter.

"Wait!" Maya yelled, breaking her serene demeanor. She stood from the bed, and her green silk dress complemented her gait as she glided over to Elyk and Akirrel. The atmosphere in the chamber crackled with tension as she intervened. "Akirrel, why must you do this time and time again? Why do you torture yourself so?"

Akirrel locked eyes with her. "I thought you loved me...

once, long ago. But your betrayal is far deeper than Elyk's. You're the reason I suffer so. You're the reason I've come back time and time again!"

"I saved you when you died the first time. I couldn't stop Elyk from killing you, but the magic of reincarnation allowed you to survive. I had no choice but to stay with Elyk. He had plans, and I wanted to be a part of them. After all this time, I thought you would have understood I gave you this gift so you could still be you, regardless of how things ended. You would be lost like the other mortals, returning to nothing and losing everything that makes them who they are. I care about you, Akirrel." Maya reached for his face with a gentle touch as he struggled to pull away.

"Is it thanks you desire?" He almost laughed himself to insanity. "Maya, I loved you, and you returned that love by cursing me! Death after death brings me no peace. I awaken to see my last moments before Elyk took his sword and struck me down as you watched, doing nothing. The first death thousands of years ago still seems as though it happened only days past."

"Enough!" Elyk's eyes gazed upon Akirrel. "It ends now. This spell you spoke of, Akirrel, I've gained it myself. Whenever you're born, my people are already watching. Whatever you try to do, one of my agents takes every detail. It didn't have to be like this, but you were always stubborn. These silly notions of justice and honor only dimmed your view of the possibilities before us. The years you've wasted fueled by jealousy and anger show how petty of a creature you truly are."

"No. Your true death would bring about a world of people realizing they can exist without tyranny." Akirrel eyed the blade Elyk held as it moved closer to his neck.

"Then it is a shame this world will never know a single day and night without me." Elyk took the blade and brought it down with a swift and decisive motion, intending to end Akirrel's eternal struggle.

* * * *

"Lerrika! Where are you?!" Sanda yelled throughout their home. Her voice carried well as she grew accustomed to yelling for her daughter's presence.

"I'm in my room, Mother! Where else would I be?" Lerrika responded with a voice equally broadcast, tinged with frustration at having her writing interrupted. She was near the end of the epic tale she had concocted and wanted to finish it with a finale worthy of praise from future generations. She found this task the most difficult and took her time tying everything together.

Sanda entered Lerrika's room, pleasantly surprised to see it was neatly kept more than the last time she had entered. "Still working on your novel?"

"Yes. I'm having trouble finishing it. I'm not sure what to do." Lerrika stood from the chair to the computer terminal. Pacing was a habit she had gotten from her father, Danjo.

"Must you pace?" Sanda placed a set of washed laundry into one of her daughter's drawers.

"It helps me to think, Mother. I need to move to think." Lerrika explained.

"Some fresh air would do the same. How about we go for a walk? You can get this pacing out of your system, and I can be even more sane for not witnessing you do so inside this house." Sanda suggested.

"Where would you like to walk to?" Lerrika stopped moving.

"We go to wherever our feet take us, my darling daughter. A lot of writers liked to walk," Sanda said.

Lerrika's skepticism showed. "Name a few."

"I'm no expert on the subject, but I gather all those who could walk really enjoyed it." Sanda smiled while giving her daughter a wink.

"Oh, you're just filled with jokes today, aren't you, Mother?" Without hesitation, Lerrika grabbed her mother's hand and allowed her to escort her down the stairs of their home. Though she was in her early teen years, she still enjoyed acting as a child many years younger from time to time.

As they stepped outside to the foreign terrain of another planet, the air was crisp and carried the scent of alien plant life unique to Iltej. The colony, surrounded by a protective energy field, stood against the backdrop of unfamiliar landscapes. Lerrika and Sanda strolled along the path, the cool breeze rustling the leaves of exotic trees.

"Tell me more about your novel, Lerrika. What's the grand finale you're pondering?" Sanda asked, enjoying the walk and the chance to engage with her daughter.

Lerrika considered. "Well, I'm torn between two possibilities. One is a triumphant resolution with the hero overcoming all odds, and the other is a bittersweet ending with sacrifices made for the greater good. I want it to be memorable, you know?"

"That's quite a choice. Both have merit. What does your heart tell you?" Sanda inquired, glancing at her daughter with maternal warmth.

Lerrika pondered momentarily, looking out at the alien landscape stretching before them. "I think... I want it to resonate with hope. Even while facing challenges, the characters find hope and strength to move forward. Maybe that's what our walk today will help me discover."

Sanda smiled, proud of her daughter's thoughtful approach to storytelling. They continued their walk, the vibrant hues of Iltej's flora painting a picturesque backdrop to their conversation.

* * * *

The central base camp in Iltej bustled with an overflow of life. Ground cars drove through the streets transporting people and goods; hovercrafts zoomed from building to building above. In the far distance, at the spaceport, off-world transports ascended and descended in the afternoon sky.

Lerrika enjoyed these constitutionals she took with her mother. They relaxed her and allowed her to spend time with the woman in a way that was not embarrassing. She was getting older now, and the childish things her mother did weren't fitting for a woman. It was a hard lesson, but one Lerrika trudged through with the angst of any teenager.

"I remember how things were before all of this was built," Sanda remarked, looking at her surroundings as they walked at a leisurely pace. "I helped draft some designs for the vehicles we use, along with how the waste in the city is reprocessed."

"I know, Mother. You remind me of the fact every time we step outside," Lerrika said, knowing she would have to hear the story again.

"Well, I'm sorry for being proud of my work, my darling daughter. We've built ourselves a society here. It's far away from the original planets, where vicious wars rage. It stifles me to think that as technologically savvy as we've become as a race, we still can act as barbaric as ever. People always feud. It never fails. Even here in Iltej, though, it's a lot more low-key and political. I gather it has turned from physical to intellectual — the wars. You should write your next story about that," Sanda sighed, wondering if any of her words resonated with her daughter.

"I viewed something on the holo newscast. They said a treaty had been signed and that peace was eminent with some of the feuding worlds." Lerrika did her best to partake in this conversation with her mother. It seemed important somehow.

"We can only hope, my darling daughter," Sanda sighed once again and descried red lights flashing off in the distance. The sight of the glow created a knot in her stomach that reached to her throat, making her want to vomit. Sirens soon followed the lights, and she understood what would be next. "No... The protective shields have been disabled..."

"Why are the sirens sounding, Mother?" Lerrika was at a loss. The sirens blared. A mass wave of panicked colonists rushed around in sporadic directions.

"We have to find shelter!" Without thinking, Sanda grabbed Lerrika by the arm, dragging her across the main square of the base camp to the nearest building with a deep underground subsection.

"Why aren't we going home? I'm scared! Where's Father?" Lerrika couldn't hold back the tears of fear as she viewed the red ships covering the blue skies above. From those ships, small spherical shapes descended at terminal velocity. Even a young teenage girl understood ships like that could only drop one thing.

"No! It can't end this way!" Sanda stopped running, knowing they would never find shelter in time. *Peace was a lie! The bastards planned this attack!*

Sanda held her daughter tight as tears fell. They witnessed in shocked horror as a red sphere made contact on the ground near them, and...

* * * *

Aki R. Rel stood before the computer terminal in the student lab, slamming his fists on the console. Frustrated beyond words, he turned off the Iltej program and forced himself to walk away from the terminal before kicking the contraption with all his might.

"What's the matter now?" Jeffers asked, sitting only two terminals down. It was crunch time at the university, and Jeffers and Aki always waited until the last minute to complete assignments. "Did your program crash on you again, Rel?" Jeffers always called him by his last name, knowing how much Aki hated his first name.

"My senior thesis revolves around an AI program that can determine a pattern of humanity that will live in peace with the fruit of technology to assist. The program comprises a replica of our society. And the technology is 'inspired' to individuals in the vast program by me. Technology is supposed to make every-one's lives better, but the people in the program keep using it for war, to conquer, and to kill. No matter what I do, it evolves into complete chaos. Utopia just can't exist, can it? Not even in an AI program." Aki explained.

"Maybe it's time to change your thesis to the opposite of what you intended. The program appears to support the contrary argument." Jeffers continued fixing a glitch in his program.

Aki paced back and forth in the small space before his computer terminal. "The little girl died."

"What?" Jeffers stopped what he was doing and turned his chair to face Rel; Rel paced back and forth. It annoyed him how much Rel paced when thinking. "What do you mean?"

"A little girl was in the program; she was a teenager. I grew kind of fond of her. Her name was Lerrika. She was a bright kid. She had a brilliant future in that program, and she died because a peace treaty was broken. Her world was invaded and destroyed." Aki sighed and sat down, slumping into his chair.

"Look, Rel, I know you get into what you do, but you have to remember, no matter how real these programs seem, they're not. She was never alive; therefore, she couldn't have died." Jeffers explained, sympathy in his voice.

"What is death, Jeffers? How do we even know we're alive?" Aki remembered the story he viewed Lerrika working on. The main character, Akirrel, was about to die for good, but now he would never find out the ending.

"Who knows, Rel? I know we're here and now and need to make the best of it. We need to do that, although your AI program doesn't want to be a peace-loving one. By nature, humanity is prone to violence and suffering. It's sad, but in the end, that's how we define ourselves. Violence is a byproduct. People gravitate to it because they become important when they have someone's life in their hands. Nothing will change this unless we experience some kind of conscious evolution as a people; it needs to be an emotional and psychological evolution." Jeffers rubbed his eyes, experiencing the exhaustion of the past six hours.

"Never had a clue you were so philosophical." Aki turned to his screen. "What if we're just figments of someone's imagination like the people in these programs are to us? What if someone is writing out every little detail we do and deciding whether we live and die, even though we think we're in control of every choice we make?"

"And I'm the one being philosophical?" Jeffers chuckled.

Aki shrugged. "I'm just saying, Jeffers - just throwing it out there."

Jeffers nodded. "I know, and someone is writing our story."

"And who would that be?" Aki smirked.

"Probably some asshole in a chair who spilled his coffee while writing on one of those antique wireless keyboards." Jeffers laughed. "Can you imagine? How crazy would it be if we were just characters in a story?"

Aki chuckled while looking over his program. He needed to find a solution to his problem or develop a new senior thesis to fit into the context of his existing program. The clock was ticking, with only twelve hours left.

THINGS UNSPOKEN

STORY 15

HE SEALED THE door from within the cargo bay, a cold, impenetrable barrier leaving Commander Jimenez speechless. She stared through the plate glass porthole, her gaze locked onto Captain Duarte, who took laborious breaths, drawing life from the dwindling oxygen reserves of the faltering life support systems. The Neknur floated in the unforgiving expanse of space, its life support systems in shambles, particularly within the sealed-off cargo hold. Captain Duarte made the ultimate sacrifice, a testament to his unwavering determination to safeguard his remaining crew. Powerless, the crew beheld their leader as he succumbed to the inevitable.

"Captain," Jimenez reined in her emotions, her voice trembling with desperation. "We must find a way to rescue you."

"You understand doing so would imperil us all," Duarte's voice quivered, transmitted through the overhead speakers —

their only means of connection in this dire moment. "Opening this door would spell doom for every soul on board. It must remain sealed from within. We have no alternative and no time for anything else."

Jimenez clenched her fists, her anger and despair boiling over. "You should have granted us more time to seek a solution!"

"Pull yourself together!" Duarte snapped, his voice carrying an urgency that drained more of his precious energy than he intended. His eyes bore the weight of profound regret as they locked onto Mara through the porthole. "You're in charge now."

The Neknur bore the scars of a harrowing collision with space debris, transforming the once-majestic vessel into a drifting object lost amidst the cosmic rubble. It moved languidly through the void, its distress beacon a desperate plea for help, whether from human or alien hands (although contact with aliens was yet to occur, if ever). The distance to the nearest base loomed insurmountable, an abyss of drift and despair — until the Captain made his resolute decision. The rest of the crew owed their lives to his sacrifice.

"The collision created too many breaches, Mara. We didn't have sufficient time to seal them all. We're a mere skeleton crew aboard an antiquated ship. We lacked the proper equipment, and sealing this door from your position outside the cargo bay was impossible. It couldn't be done in the manner needed from there. You understand this, and so do the rest of the crew," Duarte's breaths grew labored with each spoken word.

Mara Jimenez longed to cry out, to hold him, to convey the depth of her feelings. Aboard this civilian ship, their dynamic remained that of a family - a husband and wife. She represented more than his first-in-command. Over the years, much was left unspoken. Mara relied on the foolish and unwavering belief that tomorrow would always come.

"Why didn't you give me more time?" It was the only question she summoned the strength to ask.

Duarte's eyes grew heavier as he gasped for breath. "You

shouldn't be here for this," he whispered, sinking to the cargo hold's floor, perched on the ship's outer rim. "I need to sit down now," he muttered, his voice faltering. "Don't watch me die. I don't want you to witness it. The pain of it - it would be too much."

"It's already excruciating." Tears flowed as she pressed her hand against the glass. With a sudden surge of frustration, she struck the tempered glass with a fierce fist, her knuckles splitting open, a trickle of blood smearing the see-through barrier. "Damn you!"

Memories inundated her consciousness — a time when they still walked the Earth, their dreams of venturing among the stars mere possibilities. They had been so young, so brimming with hope for the boundless future that awaited them, anticipating the adventures ahead.

Captain Duarte, youthful and eager, gazed at his long-time lover as they stood in the backyard of their newly acquired country abode, their eyes locked on the stars above. "What kind of ship do you think suits a guy like me?"

"You can make any ship work, babe. That's why you're destined to be an amazing captain," Mara smiled, her voice tinged with affection. "I just want the opportunity to conduct our research and set everything in motion."

"No need to fret over that. Our chance will come," he assured her. "I can hardly wait, Mara. I'm eager to journey among the stars with you by my side and a capable crew to support us. Who knows what awaits us in the vast expanse of the cosmos? Endless possibilities." Duarte turned to her with an indelible smile.

"Hopefully, we'll uncover more solutions than questions. Maybe even lay our hands on that elusive Nobel Prize we've daydreamed about," she chuckled. Winning such a prestigious award seemed far-fetched, but in the recesses of her mind, she couldn't help but entertain the possibility. After all, their research was poised to be at the cutting edge of discovery.

Mara's fingers traced the porthole; each touch reminded Mara of their journey, echoing every step leading to this pivotal moment. Both of them understood their unspoken feelings, yet fear kept their emotions buried beneath the weight of their work. This pattern defined their relationship, always leaving their state of mind unspoken, submerged in the relentless pursuit of their mission. They found solace in their work, immersing themselves in endless theories and discussions, avoiding the uncharted territory of their hearts.

The perils of space were as genuine as they came, even for civilian space crews. In the unknown expanse, anything could happen, often resulting in the unexpected loss of comrades. Bonds were forged, but attachment was a luxury they couldn't afford. It was a lesson Mara Jimenez failed miserably at this juncture in her life.

"Do you remember... the first time I laid eyes on you?" His voice trembled. Every word became a struggle as he wiped the sweat from his forehead, his hand making a feeble sound as it met the metal floor.

"Yes. I was wandering on campus, lost in thought. It was during my first week, and I wasn't paying attention to my surroundings. I tripped over someone lying on the grass." Tears flowed from her eyes as she reminisced, a mixture of laughter and grief.

"More like crashed onto me," he managed a chuckle, his breaths growing shallower. "It hurt like hell when you landed."

"You shouldn't have been lounging in the middle of a walking path," she chided, futilely attempting to wipe away the tears. "It was your own fault, you know."

"I'm glad it happened." It grew more difficult to smile.

Mara nodded. "Me too." She continued. "I remember the first time I saw you in uniform. CryoTech's maiden civilian space fleet. You looked incredibly handsome," she recalled, an image etched in her mind of Tom Duarte emerging from the bathroom in the early morning light, clad in the blue uniform. He had been leaner back then, and the two-piece attire hugged his masculine form to perfection. He embodied the ideal of what CryoTech aimed to achieve.

CryoTech... S.A.M. The mission.

Mara clung to the memory of the first time she saw him in that uniform.

CryoTech... S.A.M. The mission.

Still clad in the nightgown from the previous evening, Mara rushed towards Tom and leaped into his waiting arms, her face lighting up with an affectionate grin. "Hey, handsome. I've always carried a soft spot for a man in uniform."

Tom returned her smile. "What can I say? I clean up nice,"

She slapped his cheek with playfulness as he set her down. "Don't get too cocky."

Tom soaked in the image of her from head to toe. "I can't wait to see you in yours."

Mara chuckled, her playful demeanor giving way to a touch of uncertainty. "Well, I have received no official invitation to join the crew, and CryoTech hasn't offered me a position either."

"You'll have a position," Tom reassured her, eyeing himself in a full-length mirror. "I requested you."

"The request guarantees nothing, babe." Mara sighed, perching herself back on the bed. "Doesn't it even trouble you that CryoTech is bankrolling this entire venture?"

Tom considered her question. "No, why should it?"

"They're a global conglomerate responsible for S.A.M., pioneers in perfecting A.I. as we know it. Their primary business revolves around cryogenically preserving people in suspended animation for extended periods. What's their vested interest in space exploration? Do you even trust this S.A.M. program that's integrated into every facet of SMART technology?" She let the thoughts troubling her spill out without regard for consequence.

"S.A.M. has improved life for most of us. The ones who are willing to accept it that is. As for what CryoTech plans... Who knows, hon? My first guess would be colonization. The idea of escaping Mother Earth doesn't seem all that bad. And if things go well, there's a fortune to be made. CryoTech has a knack for such ventures. Their expertise in cryogenic preservation will en-able ships to traverse vast distances without the crew aging and succumbing before they reach their destination. We may be children of Earth, but eventually, every mother has to let go." Tom quoted CryoTech's space travel slogan, fully aware that it irritated Mara.

"The events unfolding, don't they bother you?" she probed. "Isn't it troubling that a conglomerate like CryoTech is currently running world governments? People wishing to remain independent have made it clear they want nothing to do with artificial intelligence known as S.A.M."

"Are you referring to the terrorist groups rising as of late?" Tom inquired.

Mara sighed. "I suppose you could call them that."

"What else would you call them? They target CryoTech and S.A.M. facilities. Innocent lives have been lost in their attacks. The global police force is justified in locking them up without too many questions. That's my take." He freely admitted.

Mara couldn't help but ponder about S.A.M. *Is this artificial intelligence any less of a threat than those opposing it?*

"You didn't look too shabby the first time I saw you in uniform, either. But then again, you've always looked good wearing anything. You have always been beautiful." Tom's words interrupted her thoughts, returning her to the painful reality aboard the Neknur.

"Save your strength, Tom," she whispered. It was the first time she had used his first name in ages. Throughout their service on the ship, she had grown accustomed to addressing him as Captain Duarte, only occasionally using his last name during the intimate moments in their private cabin.

"There's nothing left to save. There was so much I wanted to say... I never found the right words," Tom declared with a herculean effort. He rose and moved to the plate glass porthole, gazing upon Mara one last time. Their eyes locked, and Mara's deep brown eyes were precisely what he wished to hold on to during his final moments.

"Tom..." she whispered.

"I'm glad, in my last moments, I can take comfort in knowing you'll be okay." He pushed his remaining strength into the brightest smile he could muster.

With those words, Tom's body fell to the cold steel floor of the cargo hold. His breaths grew fainter, and his eyes rolled back. The proud Captain Tom Duarte was reduced to an empty vessel, no longer fueled by the passions of life. The void he left behind weighed on Mara as she beheld his lifeless form becoming just another inanimate object in the cargo hold.

"I love you," the words escaped Mara's lips as she gazed upon his body. No more tears streamed down her cheeks, and no more sobs racked her body. A profound numbness engulfed her, a sensation like no other, settling into every fiber of her being.

Over the speakers, the voice of one of her bridge officers interrupted her reverie. "Commander Jimenez, the Chief wants to share her plans on how to proceed with rerouting power."

The numbness consumed her.

"Commander Jimenez?" The bridge officer's voice cracked through the speakers again.

"Tell the Chief I'll be there shortly." Duty beckoned, lives hung in the balance, and her role allowed no time for mourning. There would be ample time for grief once they returned to Earth.

As she traversed the corridor, thoughts of their precious cargo occupied her mind. Tom's closeness to her made him oblivious to the smuggling onboard the Neknur.

The rise of S.A.M. disturbed the balance of power across the world. A unified government under the control of the mighty artificial intelligence dictated every aspect of human life. She was one of the few who fought against such mindless control. Little by little, the cold calculations of the machine entity stripped away humanity. It sought to protect, but by doing so, it removed choice.

Choice is what makes us who we are. Mara thought. She had chosen to fight for a free humanity and used her status in CryoTech as a means to an end.

The device would be implemented as a countermeasure. Its construction took place on the dark side of the moon. A long-forgotten colony outpost now served as a home base to the people seeking to be released from S.A.M.'s grasp.

We're using a program integrated with an actual human mind to fight a program created by humans. Mara prayed it was the correct decision. If all went well, the two monstrosities would annihilate one another. What they carried onboard the Neknur would serve to corrupt and dismantle S.A.M. once and for all.

Tom was next to it the entire time. He didn't even understand why I wanted to ensure the breach was sealed. It wasn't to save the crew. I wanted to ensure the modified suspended animation module didn't get blown into space. We need it. The guilt intensified, but she fought it back. Tom was one life compared to the billions doomed to S.A.M. Once connected to the network S.A.M. controlled, the human mind connected to the module and the rogue A.I. would attack, hopefully taking S.A.M. by surprise.

CryoTech... S.A.M. The mission.

Relief washed over her as she contemplated the potential salvation it offered against the looming threat of S.A.M.

CryoTech... S.A.M. The mission.

Tom never uncovered her true motives, and now he never would. He would never know that she was taking desperate measures to ensure the survival of their unborn child.

I never told him; she fought back the guilt with cold determination. Pregnancy in space was not uncommon with the long tours and mixed crews, but it also presented a unique set of dangers.

CryoTech... S.A.M. The mission.

She was fighting for their unborn child. Mara learned of the pregnancy two days prior. She had meant to tell him. She always wanted the time to be right. Now, there was no more time.

CryoTech... S.A.M. The mission.

In the eyes of the global police force, she was branded a terrorist, but in her own heart, she viewed herself as a patriot and champion of a free humanity - one no longer under the pressing hand of S.A.M.

To Tom - to the memory of their relationship - it all fell under the category of things unspoken.

Be careful what you wish for...

You might find it at reality's edge...

www.ingramcontent.com/pod-product-compliance
Lightning Source LLC
Chambersburg PA
CBHW072354020726
47506CB00004B/1111